ARCHIE GOODWIN—
WITNESS TO MURDER!

As I lifted my foot for the first step up to our door, two men came out of the dark corner behind the stone wall of the stoop. The one on the left was Dazy Perrit.

"I want to ask you about tonight," Perrit said. "My car's around the corner. Go ahead. We'll come behind."

I decided to stand pat. "I like it—" I started, and stopped, hearing the sound of a car coming. I turned my head to look, because the sound of a car coming got on my nerves after my recent experience with it. But it was only a taxicab.

I turned back to them. "I like it here. Even if I had ideas, which I haven't, my gun's empty, so relax. I emptied it—"

I didn't duck or dive, I just dropped flat on the sidewalk and started rolling. I didn't see the man in the taxicab at all, I was moving too fast, rolling to get around the corner.

A NERO WOLFE THREESOME

TROUBLE IN TRIPLICATE
BY REX STOUT

BANTAM BOOKS · TORONTO · LONDON · NEW YORK

TROUBLE IN TRIPLICATE

*A Bantam Book | published by arrangement with
The Viking Press, Inc.*

PRINTING HISTORY
*Viking edition published February 1949
Dollar Mystery Guild edition published September 1951
Bantam edition published September 1951
New Bantam edition published November 1955*
2nd printing .. December 1955   3rd printing ...... May 1967
New Bantam edition published June 1974

Acknowledgment is made to THE AMERICAN MAGAZINE, *in which
these short novels originally appeared; the magazine
title for* Instead of Evidence *was* Murder on Tuesday.

CONTENTS

1 | Before
      I Die

I

THAT Monday afternoon in October, life indoors was getting to be more than I cared to take.
Meaning, by indoors, the office of Nero Wolfe, where I
worked, on the ground floor of the house he owned on
West Thirty-fifth Street not far from North River. Relief
was due soon, since he spent two hours every afternoon,
from four to six, with the orchids up in the plant rooms
on the roof, but it was still thirty minutes short of four
o'clock and I had had all of him I could stand for a
while.

I wasn't blaming him; I was merely fed up with him.
It was smack in the middle of the Great Meat Shortage,
when millions of pigs and steers, much to the regret of
the growers and slaughterers, had sneaked off and hid
in order to sell their lives dear, and to Nero Wolfe a
meal without meat was an insult. His temper had got so
bad that I had offered to let him eat me, and it would
be best to skip his retort. By that Monday afternoon he
had got so desperate that he had started taking long
walks, as, for instance, back and forth between his chair
and the bookshelves, and sometimes even through the
door into the front room, which faced on Thirty-fifth
Street.

So at three-thirty I told him I was going out for an
errand down the street, and he was sunk so far in
misery and malice that he didn't even demand to know
what the errand was. Then, just as I was reaching for
my hat on the rack in the hall, the doorbell rang. I let
the hat wait, stepped to the door and opened it, and
what I saw jerked my mind loose from the fastenings

1

where it had got glued onto Wolfe's huff. Standing there on the stoop was one of the most obvious articles I had ever looked at. Though the sun had been shining all day and still was, he had on a raincoat, belted tight. His hat, a glossy black felt number, was too small for him, and it looked out of place for the lids of his light gray eyes to be open because his face was embalmed—or, at least, after he had breathed his last and had been embalmed, his face would look exactly the way it looked now.

"Your name's Goodwin," he told me impolitely, without overexerting any muscles.

"Thanks," I thanked him. "How much do I weigh?"

But he was serious-minded. "Come on out." He jerked a thumb backwards. "Guy here in a car wants to see you."

I pause for character identification, wanting to make it clear that I neither scream with fear nor start pulling the trigger every time I see a stranger with an embalmed face reach in his pocket for a cigarette. But in his long career as a private detective Nero Wolfe has aroused many emotions in many people, some of them tenacious, and since I have been employed by him for over ten years my name is undoubtedly on a few lists along with his. So I told the face to hold it a minute, stepped back inside and swung the door shut, went to the office and across to my desk, opened a drawer and took a gun, and put it in my side coat-pocket, leaving my hand there.

As I was heading back for the hall Wolfe demanded peevishly, "What is it? A mouse?"

"No, sir," I said coldly. "I was asked to descend to the sidewalk to approach a man in a car. The car is at the curb. I recognized the man in it as Dazy Perrit. Since he is one of our most famous citizens I suppose you may have heard of him. His latest title is King of the Black Market. He may have formed an opinion, contrary to yours, that I would be good broiled."

I went. Outdoors on the stoop, after shutting the door and hearing the lock click, I took my hand from my pocket to show the face what was in it, put it back in the pocket, descended the steps to the sidewalk, and crossed to the car, a big black sedan. The man inside cranked the window down.

From behind my right shoulder a voice was saying, "He's got his hand on a gun in his pocket."

"Then he's damn silly," the man in the car said through the window, "to let you behind him."

"Huh-uh." I looked through at Dazy Perrit. It all depended on the conversation. "Mr. Wolfe knows you're here. What do you want?"

"I want to see Wolfe."

"I shook my head. "Nope." I was ignoring the hired man. This was the closest I had ever been to Dazy Perrit. To most people he would have seemed a big fat man, but to me, used as I was to the magnitude of Nero Wolfe, he was merely rounded out. His face, smooth and shaved to the pink, was too big for his nose and mouth, but that was unimportant on account of the eyes. Everything he had done and might do was in his black eyes.

"Nope," I said. "I told you on the phone this morning that Mr. Wolfe is too busy to see you. He's got more work than he can handle now."

"I intend to see him. Go in and tell him."

"Lookit, mister." I put an elbow on the window sill and leaned in to him. "Don't think I'm laughing you off. People who laugh you off are apt to show up soon at a funeral, playing the lead. Okay. But neither am I asking any favors. Whatever you have in mind, and you're being pretty damn stubborn about it, Mr. Wolfe wants no part of it. That may make you sore, which would be a pity and should be avoided if possible, but not half as sore as you would be if you rolled something out in front of him and let him look and then he didn't like it. That would be really bad, either for him or for you, and don't be too sure—"

"Archie!"

It was a bellow from my right rear. I straightened and wheeled, and saw the upper half of Wolfe filling the space left by a window he had opened—the rear window of the front room.

He bellowed again, "What does Mr. Perrit want?"

"Nothing," I called. "He just stopped by—"

"He wants to see you," the face put in.

3

"Then confound it, Archie, bring him in here!"

"But I—"

"Bring him in!"

The window banged shut and Wolfe was gone. The face looked searchingly up and down the street, and across, then reached past me to open the door of the car, and Dazy Perrit climbed out.

II

I decided I didn't know as much about underworld royalty as I thought I did. Surely the thing would have been for the hired man to come along, watching for treachery in all directions at once, but Dazy Perrit told him to stay by the car and entered the house alone with me. Two paces inside the office he stopped to make a survey, probably merely through force of habit, like a veteran general playing golf on a strange course automatically picking out the best spots to place artillery units or hide his tanks. I walked on past him and sat down at my desk, warning myself not to underestimate his potentialities just because he was six inches shorter than me. I was too sore at Wolfe to speak.

"Be seated, sir," Wolfe said graciously.

Perrit had finished surveying the premises and was surveying Wolfe. After five seconds he spoke as if he were a little irritated. "I don't like it in here. I've got something private for you. Come out and sit in my car."

I was really on edge because I was sure Wolfe would make himself obnoxious, and getting obnoxious with Dazy Perrit simply had no percentage. But Wolfe said, "My dear sir," and chuckled in a friendly manner. "I rarely leave my house. I do like it here. I would be an idiot to leave this chair, made to fit me—"

"I know, I know," Perrit said impatiently. He aimed the black eyes at me. "*You* go out and sit in my car."

"No, sir," Wolfe said emphatically. "Do be seated. That red leather chair is the best one. I do nothing without Mr. Goodwin. If you confided in me, no matter what, under a pledge of confidence, I would tell it all to him as soon as you left."

"You might make exceptions. I might be a good exception to start with."

"No, sir." Wolfe was courteous but firm. "Sit down, Mr. Perrit. Even if you decide against trusting secrets to Mr. Goodwin and me, there's a little matter I'd like to discuss with you."

Perrit was no hummer and hawer. He took three steps to the red leather chair near the end of Wolfe's desk, lowered himself into it, and asked, "What do you want to discuss?"

"Well." Wolfe's eyes went half shut. "In my own field I am an expert, and I sell expert information, advice, and services. I am not intimately acquainted with your activities, but I understand that you are also an expert—uh, in a different field. Presumably you know where certain things are and how they may be got. I am on the whole a respectable and virtuous citizen, but like everyone else I have my smudges. Where is some meat?"

"Oh." Perrit sounded chilly. "Maybe I've got you lined up wrong. You want a slice of the meat racket?"

"No. I want slices of beef and pork. I want some meat to eat. Lamb. Veal."

So that was it. I gazed at my boss in bitter disgust. He had lost all sense of proportion. For the sake of making a wild grab for a rib roast, he had left his chair, walked clear to the front room, opened a window and invited the most deadly specimen between the Battery and Yonkers into his house.

"Oh," Perrit said, not so cool, "you're just hungry."

"Yes, I am."

"That's too bad. I'm not a butcher and I'm not a retailer. In fact I'm not in meat at all. But I'll see—" He broke it off and looked at me as if I was the butler. "Ring Lincoln six-three two three two, between seven and ten in the morning and ask for Tom and use my name."

"Thank you, sir." Wolfe was as sweet as stick candy. "I assure you this is appreciated. Now for your own business. Mr. Goodwin told you on the phone this morning that I was too busy to see you. Of course that was flummery. What was in his mind was that while the occupational hazards are relatively high in the detective business, in your business—that is to say, in any activity connected with you—they are substantially higher, and a combination of the two would be inadvisable. I must admit, regretfully, that I agree with him. It would be foolish for you to entrust me with secrets only to be told that I can't undetake a job for you, so I tell you in advance. I'm sorry."

"I need help," Perrit said.

"Doubtless, or you wouldn't have—"

"I don't often need help. When I do I get the best there is. I like everything the best. For what I need now, I've picked you as the best. I pay for what I get." Perrit took from his breast pocket a neat little stack of bills, unfolded, held with a rubber band, and tossed it onto Wolfe's desk. "Fifty C's. Five grand. That will do for a start. I'm being blackmailed and your job is to stop it."

I goggled at him. The idea of Dazy Perrit being pestered by a blackmailer was about the same as Billy Sunday being pestered by an evangelist trying to convert him.

"But I've told you, Mr. Per—"

"I'm being blackmailed by my daughter. That's one thing nobody in the world knows except me, and now you and this man of yours. Here's another thing, and this is even more particular. This is very particular. I wouldn't tell it to my mother even if I still had one, but I need help. My daughter is—"

"Hold it!"

Dazy Perrit was not easy to stop, but I made it positive enough to stop him. I was out of my chair, standing in front of him. "I want to warn you," I told his eyes, "that Mr. Wolfe is fully as stubborn as you are. This is damn dangerous business for all concerned. He's told you he doesn't want to hear it, and neither do I!" I turned savagely to Wolfe. "Good God, what's wrong with spaghetti and cheese?" I picked up the stack of bills and stuck them out at Perrit.

He ignored it. His eyes hadn't even shifted to me. He went on to Wolfe, "The particular thing is that my daughter isn't really my daughter—the one that's blackmailing me, I mean. Now you know that too, you and this man. I said that nobody else in the world knows it, but she does. I have got a daughter, born in nineteen

6

twenty-five, twenty-one years ago. She'll be twenty-one next month, November eighth. There's a job for you to do with her too. What's up?"

"You'll have to excuse me, Mr. Perrit." Wolfe had glanced at the wall clock, pushed his chair back from the desk, and was manipulating his bulk upright. He moved from behind the desk and then stopped, because Perrit, also on his feet, was standing square in his path.

"Where you going?" Perrit asked in a tone which implied that no conceivable answer would be acceptable.

I stood up too, my hand leaving my pocket with the gun in it—that is, in my hand. That may strike some as corny, but it was instinctive and the instinct was sound. I got around town some and was fairly well informed, and so far as I knew no serious argument with Dazy Perrit had ever been settled with any tool but a gun; and up to then Perrit had done all the settling, either personally or by staff work. With what he had already spilled I could see nothing ahead but one fine mess, and I still believe, corn or no corn, that if he had so much as poked a finger at Wolfe's central bulge I would have dropped him.

But Wolfe said, unperturbed. "I always spend from four to six upstairs with my plants. Always. If you insist on confiding your troubles to me, tell Mr. Goodwin about it. I'll phone you this evening or in the morning."

The point was settled, not with words, but with eyes. Wolfe's eyes won. Perrit moved a step to the right. Wolfe went on by and out, and a moment later the bang of the door on his personal elevator sounded.

Perrit sat down and told me, "You're crazy. Both of you. What's that thing in your hand for? Crazy as bedbugs."

I put the gun on the desk and heaved a sigh. "Okay, tell me about it."

III

At one point I thought Dazy Perrit was going to break down and cry. That was when he was telling me that his daughter, his real daughter, was up among the top of her class at Columbia. Apparently that made him feel so proud he could hardly bear it.

It wasn't really very complicated. In his early days in St. Louis Perrit had got married and there was a daughter. Then three things happened in the same week: the daughter had her second birthday, the mother died, and Perrit got three years in the hoosegow for a stick-up. I got only a rough sketch of this and practically nothing of the years that followed, up to 1945; all he gave me was that somewhere along the line, when he had begun to get prosperous, he had got daughter-conscious and had dug her up somewhere in Missouri. He didn't say where or how he had got her away, but in order to give me the picture he had to explain that she didn't know she was his daughter. She thought he was merely representing her father, who was very wealthy and couldn't disclose himself because he was planning to get elected President of the United States or something.

"It was okay," Dazy Perrit said sourly. "It was working fine. I saw her about every three months and gave her money. Plenty. It was a break for me when she picked a school right here in town. Then Thumbs Meeker bitched it up. He sent a punk to tell me that if there was any little favor he could do for my daughter just to let him know."

That, of course, from my standpoint, made it even sweeter. Mr. Meeker, called Thumbs on account of his favorite method of getting information from reluctant persons, in which he used both thumbs, was the cave man on the other side of the mountain. If to be associated with Dazy Perrit in anything whatever was a doubtful pleasure, to be yanked in between him and Thumbs Meeker was enough to start ulcers.

I went on listening to Perrit because there was nothing else to do but shoot him, and I had missed the psychological moment for that. It appeared from developments, he said, that Meeker had not actually tagged his daughter but had merely learned that he had one concealed somewhere. But, he said, the one thing on earth he was afraid of was that someone would find his daughter and tell her the facts. That was what had ruined his life, having a daughter.

8

"It ruined me," he said, "because it put water in my guts. Where she's concerned I can't think straight and I can't act straight. You've heard I'm tough? You've heard that?"

"Yeah, I've heard it said."

"Okay, I'm tough. But there's plenty of tough ones. The point is I've got brains. I've got better brains than any man I've ever met. If I had got started on another track I could have been anything you care to name. But where she's concerned my brains don't work. Look at my coming here and spilling this. Worse yet, look at what I did a year ago April. I rented a penthouse off Fifth Avenue and brought a girl there as my daughter. I knew it was dumb but my brain wouldn't work and I did it."

That, he explained, had been for the purpose of drawing Thumbs Meeker off, and also anyone else who might be interested in the Perrit family. With his daughter living there, in the penthouse with him, naturally no one would continue searching for her other places, especially in colleges. It was a very fine arrangement. He had his secret all sewed up.

"Then," Perrit said, with a sudden change in his tone and a gleam showing in his eyes that I would not have liked at all if he had been talking about me instead of to me, "the little bitch used the pliers on me."

On that I got details, which he furnished without referring to any notes. The squeeze had started the week before Christmas with a demand for a thousand bucks cash in addition to her weekly allowance of a century. Thereafter she had requested and received:

Late January	$1500
Middle of February	1000
End of April	5000
Early in June	3000
Last of July	5000
Last of August	8000

"Interesting," I said, "how she went down, then up again, then down, then up again. Interesting psychologically."

"It strikes you as funny, does it?"

"I didn't say funny, I said interesting. And by the way, there aren't many people, I'm not saying I'm not one of them, but there are very few, who would believe a word of it. She has nicked you for nearly twenty-five grand. Why didn't she happen to have an accident, say about the third nick, like getting in the way of flying pieces of metal or something?"

"That's all exaggerated," Perrit said as if he were disappointed in me. "They start rumors and everyone believes them."

"Nuts." I grinned at him. "This is off the record, where I hope to God it stays. Why didn't you handle her or have her handled?"

"My daughter? My own daughter?"

"She wasn't. She isn't."

"As far as anyone knows she is. I would have had to do it myself, and even then it would have been very risky. She has got that all figured. What if she disappears? How would Thumbs Meeker and others dope it? I'd be right back where I started, and they'd be looking for trails again. I've looked at it from every angle and it's no go."

I shrugged. "Then you're stuck with an expensive daughter."

"I'm stuck with a glutton and a damn fool. Last night she hit me for fifty grand. That settles it. I've got to have help."

I whistled. "That takes it beyond psychology. But does she have to disappear? Why don't you try something short of curtains?"

"I have. Do you think I've shelled out with a smile?"

"No. I don't."

"Right. I haven't. But there are limits to that too, since I've got her there as my daughter. So I need help. I know lots of people, and I know a lot about lots more. I guess I must know forty or fifty lawyers, and there isn't one of them I'd spill this to or any part of it. I picked on Nero Wolfe because from what I know of him he's got brains, and mine won't work on this. It's up to Wolfe to dope out a way to handle her." He pointed at the stack of bills. "That's just for a start. I'll pay what it's worth, and it's worth plenty."

"He won't touch it."

10

Perrit ignored that completely. I was beginning to believe that the secret of his success was a gimmick on his eardrums that tuned out all unwanted sounds.

"You'll need," he said, "more than you've got if you're going to handle her. You'll need it all. Her name as my daughter is Violet Perrit. Her real name is Angelina Murphy. How I got onto her doesn't matter, but she is absolutely covered. She was on the jump in Salt Lake from a rolling and cleaning charge under the name of Sally Smith, and I went out there and got her myself. She's smooth and no disgrace. When I say my brain wouldn't work, for instance, I doped it that I'd have her sewed up because Salt Lake would like to have her back if she got tricky, but it didn't take her long to realize that I couldn't unload her."

He told me a lot more that I didn't want to know, but of course the lions were already loose and more wouldn't matter. After he finished with Violet Angelina Sally he shifted scenery and the curtain went up on Columbia. His real daughter's name was Beulah Page, and from the change in his voice when he spoke of her I fully expected him to pull out a wallet and begin showing me snapshots, but he didn't. To hear him tell it, she had the rest of the students panting along behind in a cloud of dust. He gave what seemed to be unnecessary details, which I suppose was understandable since there was no one else on earth he could tell about her, except Nero Wolfe, and Wolfe was up with his orchids and paying me to listen—though not near enough. Nothing like enough, if this ended the way I was suspecting it might.

"As I told Wolfe," Perrit said, "there's a job for him to do with my daughter too. That's another danger. There's a possibility that she might be recognized. She strongly resembles her mother."

"For God's sake," I protested, "whatever Mr. Wolfe may be, he is no plastic surgeon. Try the Red Book."

"That's funny, is it?" Perrit asked.

The words weren't much, but I admit that for the first time his tone hit me in the spine. It put him down on a lower level, and at the same time brought him a lot closer and a lot meaner. Probably members of his staff or the rank and file used it oftener than he did, now

11

that he was at the top. It was the voice of the killer. Apparently cracks about most things might pass without trouble, but no cracks about Beulah.

"Not very," I said courteously. "Better luck next time. But if you expect Mr. Wolfe to arrange for your daughter to stop resembling her mother—"

"I don't. You talk too much. She looks like her mother, but what makes it stick out is a trick she has of sitting with her shoulders down, sort of slumped forward, and then straightening up in a certain way, with a little jerk. Her mother did exactly the same thing, and the first time I saw my daughter do it, about a year ago, I saw it was a dead give-away. If anyone who knew her mother happened to see her do that, there's a good chance they would tumble. I tried to get her to stop it, as well as I could considering who I'm supposed to be, but it didn't work and I was afraid to emphasize it. I want Wolfe to get her to stop straightening up like that."

Naturally, five arguments and three or four cracks were on the tip of my tongue, but I set the brake. The only hope was to get him out of there as soon as possible, before he got in an order to tutor Beulah in math, which he had informed me was the only thing she was less than perfect in. But he wasn't ready to go, though he had spent nearly an hour with me. He had more information about Angelina Violet Sally that he thought might be helpful, suggestions about the best approach to his daughter, remarks regarding the need for immediate and effective action, and various other details. Another secret of his success, I gathered, was that he was good and thorough.

Finally he was on his feet, ready to go. "Violet," he said, "will still do what I tell her. She thinks she's going to clean me. You say Wolfe won't leave the house. If you want her down here, ring me and I'll see that she comes. You wrote down those phone numbers."

Answering not his words but his tone, I said, "You saw me put them in the safe."

"Keep 'em there. Come out and open the door and call Archie."

I stared at him. "Call who?"

"I said Archie."

12

That made the day perfect. The embalmed face's name was Archie. I took Perrit to the hall, got him his hat and coat, opened the door and stuck my head out for a look, and growled over my shoulder, "All clear. Call him yourself."

He didn't have to. My namesake, standing on the alert at the rear corner of the black sedan, had heard the door open and now crossed to the foot of the stoop steps, looked up at his employer, and announced, "Okay." Dazy Perrit descended the steps and got in the back seat of the car. The face got in front and started the engine, and they rolled off.

I went to the kitchen and poured myself a glass of milk. Fritz Brenner, the chef and groom of the chambers, was there, cutting chives into atoms. He smiled at me.

"Ca va?"

"Boy, does it *va,*" I told him, and took a gulp of milk. "The only question left is, what color shrouds do we like."

IV

I made a full and honest report to Wolfe, when he came down to the office from the plant rooms at six o'clock, only because it no longer mattered. Not only did I not want to try to persuade him to lay off, I was even afraid he might. With me crammed to the gills with Dazy Perrit's closest and fondest secrets, no kind of a brush-off would have been worth a damn. I was, if you want the facts, scared stiff. So nothing was further from my mind than trying to make Wolfe obstinate by riding him.

At seven o'clock I was telling him, "Incidentally, that Lincoln number he gave me is probably the real thing. T-bone. Chateaubriand, as Fritz calls it. Pig's liver. Fresh pork tenderloin. Of course it will be useless to ring Tom in the morning if we're not still in good with Dazy—and his five grand in our safe."

Wolfe muttered at me, "Get Mr. Perrit."

Then difficulties arose. At the third number on the list I finally got Perrit, and he said we could expect

Violet at Wolfe's office at nine o'clock that evening. It took less than twenty words, discreetly selected at both ends, with no names mentioned, to complete the conversation. Perrit could have been on a party line and no harm done. But in ten minutes he called back to say that previous engagements interfered and the visitor wouldn't arrive until eleven-thirty. I said that was pretty late and maybe tomorrow would do. No, he said, it would be tonight, between eleven-thirty and midnight.

Wolfe, who had listened in at his desk, grunted and told me, "Get the daughter."

"Violet? Or Beulah?"

"The daughter. Miss Page."

"But what the hell. There's no rush about making her stop straightening up with a jerk. That was just—"

"We don't even know there is a daughter. All we have is what Mr. Perrit told us. I want to see her. At the very least, I want you to see her."

"You going to introduce me to her?"

"Pfui. She is twenty-one years old. Flummox her."

That wasn't as much of a chore as some he had been known to give me, since Perrit had given me what he thought would be an in. I referred to the list of numbers, dialed one, and after the third buzz there was a voice in my ear.

"Hello, hello, hello?"

It didn't sound at all like a Phi Beta Kappa, but I reserved judgment and proceeded.

"May I speak to Miss Beulah Page?"

"Sure. Talking. Are you a preacher?"

"No, Miss Page, I'm not. My name is Stevens, Harold Stevens, from Dayton, Ohio. May I have a minute?"

"Sure. Only it's too bad you're not a preacher."

"It certainly is, if you want one. What I want to ask, I would like very much to have a talk with you, this evening, if possible, because I'll be in the city only a short while. I want to tell you about the Dayton Community Health Center, and, frankly, we thought you might be willing to help us out with a small contribution. You see, the fame of your generosity in matters of community health work has gone pretty far. And I'd like to tell you what we're doing and planning. I promise not to take much of your time. Perhaps I could run up to see you right now? I could be there in twenty minutes."

"I don't—" A pause. "I'm particularly interested in health work."

"I *know* you are," I said warmly.

"The reason I spoke about a preacher, I'm going to be married. We just decided to, just before the phone rang."

"Well! That's just fine! I can be there in twenty minutes. Of course I shouldn't butt in, but I won't be in the city—"

"That's all right. Come ahead. Come on and come ahead."

"Thank you *very* much."

I pushed the phone back and told Wolfe, "Lit. Not plastered, but lit."

He was busy pouring beer, which Fritz had brought, and uttered only a low growl. Nor did he make any comment as he observed me returning the gun, still lying on my desk, to my side coat-pocket, and arranging its little brother, which I got from a drawer, in an arm-pit holster of my own design.

I did not actually expect ambush and sudden death as I emerged from the house into the early October dark, but I wasn't kidding myself that any street or any two-legged animal that had become an object of interest to Dazy Perrit was exactly the same street or the same animal it had been before. And though there is absolutely nothing wrong with my nervous system, things looked and felt different as I went to the garage around the corner, got the convertible, and headed uptown.

V

In one way Perrit had given me a false impression of his daughter. I had got the idea that practically all the dough he gave her was dished out for worthy things like textbooks and health work, but it was evident that her apartment on One hundred and twelfth Street had not been furnished with spare change. The big room— and there was nothing like a bed in it, which meant

15

that wasn't all—was provided with all the articles of comfort and then some. I admit the biggest thing in it was a lacewood desk between two windows, and there was no question about her owning books.

Otherwise Perrit had her right. Her performance on the phone had given me a suspicion that Dazy was just one more male parent with wool over his eyes, but one good look at her was enough. She was no bar heifer. Me not being her father, I could face the reality that she was a little short and over-weight, but everything was there that should have been at the age of twenty-one, in its proper place, including a fairly well-arranged face with light-colored eyes totally different from dad's.

Since she had told me that they had just decided to get married when the phone rang, I was fully expecting to find the lucky man there, and there he was.

"This is Mr. Schane," Beulah told me, and he came forward for a shake. She went on, "He's been scolding me. He says I was maudlin on the phone, talking to you about a preacher. Maybe I was, but he shouldn't have got me drunk."

"Now wait a minute," Schane protested with a smile at me and then at her. "Who made the cocktails?"

"I did," she admitted, and somehow they were next to each other, touching, though neither had deliberately managed it. Evidently they were at the stage where the two organisms naturally float to a junction. She asked me, "Hasn't a girl got a right to make cocktails when she's engaged? By the way, there's a little left. Won't you have one?" She went to a table and picked up a shaker. "I'll get a glass."

"I've got a better idea," I declared, intercepting her. "I ought to be ashamed of myself for busting in on your celebration, and especially right at dinnertime. Why not let me help you go on celebrating, in a mild sort of way? How about a betrothal dinner?" I was giving them my best grin. "With no rooms in hotels, I'm putting up with a friend down on Thirty-fifth Street, and he happens to be a famous man, and also he's very hospitable. I'll call him up and tell him we're coming. All right?"

They looked at each other. "But after all," Schane objected. "We're utter strangers, not only to him but to you too."

16

"What's he famous for?" Beulah asked. "Who is he?"

"Nero Wolfe, the detective. I've known him for years. He saved my life once—uh, on a murder charge. I was innocent and he proved it."

"Oh, Morton, let's go!" Beulah had both her hands on his arm, holding him and looking up at him. "This is my first request as your bride-to-be, to come and eat dinner with Nero Wolfe! You can't refuse the first one!" She turned her head to me. "We'll make him go! He has a strong sense of propriety because he's in his last year at law school and he thinks lawyers are the guardians of everything from social conventions to moral righteousness."

"Not righteousness," Schane said firmly. "Right."

He looked it. He stood, about my height, like a bulwark against something, with a good strong chin, a face that had bones, and, just to round out the picture, dark straight-aiming eyes behind glasses in thick black frames. He said he had intended to go home and do some studying in preparation for a stiff test that was coming. She said, still holding on to his arm, surely not on their engagement evening, and when it ended the way those things always end I got permission to use the phone and crossed over to it.

Fritz's voice came. "Mr. Wolfe's residence."

"Fritz, this is Harold Stevens. . . . No, no, Mr. Wolfe's guest, Harold Stevens. May I speak to Mr. Wolfe, please?"

VI

My first chance to check on Beulah's habit that we were supposed to cure her of, sitting with her shoulders slumped and then straightening up with a jerk, came at the dinner table after Fritz had served the broiled chicken and grilled sweet potatoes. It didn't look particularly noticeable to me, but of course I didn't have the same background for it as Dazy Perrit. It would have been a cinch to kid her out of it, I thought, if she hadn't just got herself engaged. A girl who has just collared her man is not likely to be in a frame of mind to

17

be easily persuaded that anything about her needs correcting.

Her man was, in my opinion, a pain in the neck. He seemed to be under the impression that he was already married, with accumulated burdens. The food may not have been red meat but there was nothing wrong with it, as there never is when it has Fritz's by-line, and the wines were some of the best in Wolfe's cellar, but he didn't loosen up once. Law students may think they have a lot on their minds, but my God, this was a celebration of his contract for happiness. I was doing my best to keep it gay and carefree because I was afraid that if the conversation turned serious Beulah would ask me for a detailed account of the activities and plans of the Dayton Community Health Center, and that might have floored me, with her probably up on the lingo. To my surprise, Wolfe helped out by hopping all over the place, asking Beulah about her courses and other concerns, talking about himself and cases he had handled, and even trying to draw Schane out—he actually called him Morton, in a paternal tone—regarding his philosophies and ambitions.

"I don't really know anything," Morton told him while Fritz was passing the salad plates, "except law. That's the worst of a specialized education, it leaves you comparatively ignorant in all other fields. That is certainly regrettable."

"It is indeed." Wolfe reached for the bowl of dressing. "But not as regrettable as their ignorance in their own field. I hope, Morton, that you are prepared to face the fact that very few people like lawyers. I don't. They are inveterate hedgers. They think everything has two sides, which is nonsense. They are insufferable word-stretchers. I had a lawyer draw up a tort for me once, a simple conveyance, and he made it eleven pages! Two would have done it. Have they taught you to draft torts?"

Morton was too well mannered to take offense at his dinner host. "Naturally, sir, that's in the course. I try not to put in more words than necessary."

"Well, for heaven's sake, keep it brief. A little more dressing, Harold?"

I nearly muffled that one because my mind was on
18

something else. It wouldn't hurt, I thought, to make a delivery of some kind to Dazy Perrit, and in my opinion we had something to deliver. He certainly didn't know his daughter was engaged to be married, since it had just happened, and he would probably appreciate being told about it. I decided that as soon as we left the table I would excuse myself, go to my room two flights up, ring Wolfe on the house phone and get his okay, and then call Perrit from the extension in my room.

That worked all right except for the little detail that I couldn't reach Perrit. I tried all five of the numbrs he had given me, following instructions by saying it was Goodyear calling, and got nothing but not in. I left word everywhere for Perrit to call Goodyear and went downstairs to join them in the office, where they were having coffee.

Wolfe and Beulah were singing songs. At least it was as close to singing as I had ever seen him get. She was really pouring it out in words that were strangers to me, apparently songs she had mentioned at dinner that she had learned from a fellow student from Ecuador, and Wolfe was moving a finger to keep time and evidently humming. For him that was drunken revelry, and I would have merely sat and enjoyed it if I had had no worries. But it was past ten o'clock, and the situation called for my driving them home, and I didn't want to miss Violet, who might beat the gun and arrive before eleven-thirty. So I stayed on my feet.

It wasn't hard to get them out, because Morton was ready to go anyhow. Wolfe behaved like a gentleman, even getting out of his chair to say good night. I supposed that what was itching Morton was anxiety to get home and study, the wine and song having had no visible effect on him, but I was as wrong as I could be. Out at the curb, as I was opening the door of the convertible, he suddenly put his hand on my shoulder—more intimacy than I had thought him capable of in anything less than a year—and spoke.

"You know, you're a swell guy, Stevens. That was a swell idea you had. Now I've got one, and I don't think it's all the wine I drank. Or maybe it is, but so what? Whose car is this?"

"Mr. Wolfe's. He's letting me use it."

"But of course you have a driver's license?"

The damn lawyer. "Sure," I said, "I've got my license with me."

"Then, since you wanted to help us celebrate, what do you think of this? You drive us down to Maryland, it will only take four hours, and we'll get married!" He turned to Beulah, who was there against him. "How's that for an idea?"

She said promptly and emphatically, "It stinks."

"What?" He was surprised. "Why?"

"Because it does. I may not have any father or mother, or even aunts or uncles or cousins, but I don't have to sneak off to Maryland in the dead of night to get a husband. I'm going to have flowers and white things, and sunshine if I get a break. Anyway, I thought you had to study. What about that test?"

"Very well, I do have to study."

"And in case it might compromise your standing as a future Justice of the Supreme Court to be seen riding through the streets with an orphan, I've got an idea myself." Beulah was on the lope. "You can take the subway, it will get you home to your work just as quick, and Mr. Stevens and I will go somewhere and talk. Or somewhere and dance." She put a hand on my arm. "I feel guilty, Mr. Stevens, because we haven't even mentioned your Community Health Center. Couldn't we discuss that and dance at the same time?"

For a minute it looked as if I would have to crawl from under, but love found a way. The law student filed objections, motions, demurrers, and protestations, and if she had demanded a stipulation that girls with no parents shall be presumed to be descended from Julius Caesar in direct line she would probably have got it. It ended with us all piling in the convertible and heading uptown. Somewhere in the Seventies she mentioned health, and I sidetracked it by saying I'd mail her some literature which would give her the address to send a check to it she felt like it. All was serene and even cordial by the time we stopped at her address, where they both got out, and I declined an invitation to come up for a glass of something, and rolled west toward Broadway.

When I entered the office, Wolfe was seated over by

the filing cabinets, with one of the drawers open, looking over plant germination records. I sat down at my desk and asked him, "Did our client call Goodyear?"

"No."

"He's missing something. And he narrowly missed already having a son-in-law. Morton wanted me to drive them to Maryland to get tied. Tonight. She pretended that she prefers it another way, but her real reason was that now that she has met me she doesn't want him at all. She suggested he should take the subway and I should take her places. I'll have to get out of it somehow. I can't very well explain to her that I don't want Dazy Perrit for a father-in-law."

"Pfui. She's dumpy."

"Not so bad. Nothing that couldn't be adjusted." Yawning, I glanced at my wristwatch. It said eleven-fourteen. I glanced at the wall clock, a double-take habit I have been trying to get rid of for years, and it said the same.

"I wish Perrit would call," I remarked. "If we can toss him a few useful items we may get out of this alive. I admit the news that Beulah is engaged is nothing colossal, but at least it's fresh."

"We have something for him better than that," Wolfe declared.

I sent him a sharp glance because his tone had a smirk in it. "Oh? We have?"

"Yes indeed."

"Something happened while I was out?"

"No. While you were here. In your presence. Evidently you missed it."

Like that he was unbearable. When he took that attitude I never tried to pry it out of him because (a) I didn't want to feed his vanity, and (b) I knew he had decided to keep it to himself. So I considered the conversation closed, turned to my desk, elevated the typewriter, and began banging out some routine letters. I was on the fifth one when the doorbell rang.

Wolfe shut the drawer of the cabinet, arose, and started for the only chair he really loved, the one behind his desk.

"Call her Angelina," I told him as I crossed to the hall. "It'll upset her."

VII

Violet Angelina Sally sat in the red leather chair with one knee arranged over the other. Wolfe's gaze, under half-closed lids, was directed straight at her, and she was meeting it. They had been that way for full half a minute. Neither of them had spoken a word.

"Like it?" Violet asked with a high-pitched laugh.

"I was trying to decide," Wolfe muttered, "whether to let you keep the twenty-four thousand, five hundred dollars you have got from Mr. Perrit or get that from you too. At least most of it."

Violet let out a word. Ordinarily I try to report conversations without editing but we'll let that one go. Wolfe made a face. He never cares for coarse talk, but he can stand it better from men than from women.

Judging from that word, Violet talked coarser than she looked. Of an entirely different design from Beulah, with a nice long flow to her body and a face whose only objectionable characteristics were acquired, she could easily have been made an attractive number by a couple of months on the farm, with fresh eggs and milk and going to bed early. But it was obvious that she hadn't been on the farm.

"I do not intend," Wolfe said testily, no longer muttering, "to prolong this. Here's the situation. You are getting money—having already got the sum I mentioned—from Mr. Perrit by threatening to disclose the existence of his daughter. That, of course, is blackmail—"

"If you think silence gives consent," Violet put in, "you're crazy." Her voice was softer and better handled than might have been expected from her opening word.

"I'll get along without the consent for the sake of the silence," Wolfe said dryly. "As I say, that's blackmail, but I'm not concerned with the legal or criminal aspects. Your position is a little peculiar, which is often the case with blackmailers. Should Mr. Perrit call your hand and should you make the disclosure, you lose your current job and source of income. Also, since he would surely retaliate, the smallest misfortune you

22

might expect would be a jail term in Utah. So, obviously, you are convinced that he won't call your hand. I agree that it's highly unlikely. He came to me today to get help. The job is to make you stop demanding money. I took the job."

"I came down here," Violet said, "because my father told me to. I simply can't believe my ears! You say my father told you those lies? Holy Jesus, Dazy Perrit telling anyone I'm not his daughter! Now you think I believe that?"

"I think you find it difficult to believe it, Miss Murphy. Naturally. Because you calculated that Mr. Perrit, desperately anxious to keep his daughter's identity secret, would under no circumstances tell anyone that you are a counterfeit. But you misjudged his character. You didn't know, or didn't stop to consider, that his strongest feeling, stronger even than his feeling for his daughter, is his vanity. Indeed, his feeling for his daughter may be only one aspect of his vanity, but that's beside the point. He cannot, and will not, tolerate anyone's ascendancy over him. He can't stand it to have you diddle him."

Wolfe shifted to get more comfortable. "But he made the same mistake you did. He misjudged a man's character. Mine. You have demanded fifty thousand dollars from him. Henceforth, Miss Murphy, whenever you get money from Mr. Perrit, above the hundred dollars a week he allows you, you will give me ninety per cent of it—that's nine-tenths, ninety dollars from each hundred—within twenty-four hours from the moment you get it, or the Salt Lake City authorities will come and get you."

Violet stared at him. She took a breath, stared some more, and gulped. "But you—" She stopped and stared some more. Then she broke out, "You goddam fool, you can't do that to Dazy! He don't have to let you alone like he does me! All I have to do is tell him—"

She cut it off and started staring again. Suddenly the stare changed, her whole face changed. "Aw, for the love of Christ," she said contemptuously. "You think I'm that dumb? Dazy thinks I'm that dumb? I give it to you and you hand it to him and he gets off cheap,

23

wouldn't that be sweet. And he thought I would fall for that?"

She uncrossed her knees and leaned forward. "Listen," she said earnestly. "I've got what it takes, see? You think it don't take guts to face up to Dazy Perrit and make him fork it over? Wait till I show you." She began unfastening her dress. "I was at the theater tonight, but you notice I'm wearing sleeves and I'll show you why."

She had the fastenings loose and was wriggling it down from her shoulders. Down it came, revealing pink doings, and revealing also a bare arm which she extended. "What do you think of that?" she demanded.

It was quite an exhibit. The black and purple blotches began a few inches below the elbow and continued up to the shoulder curve. Curious as to what he had done it with, I got up and stepped over for a close-up, and she obligingly kept her arm up for me. I couldn't tell; it might have been fingers or fists, or he might have used something.

"That's not all," Violet said on a mixed note of pride and grievance. "There's other places, but you'd have to pay to see them. And I took it. I told him, listen, I said, if you hurt me enough, don't think I'll just go baby. You can't lock me up, you can't lock up your daughter, can you? If you hurt me enough I'll spill it plenty where it will do the most good and I'll clear out, and try and find me, you or anyone else. So you can let up, see?"

She had the dress back over her shoulders and was starting to fasten it. "He let up. I've got Dazy Perrit right, and I'm the only one that ever did that and lived to tell it. And now he thinks he can get most of it back through you with this lousy runaround!" She pronounced the word with which she had declared her position at the start.

Wolfe made another face. "But Miss Murphy." His tone was even. "You'll have to think this through. Though my assurance that Mr. Perrit and I didn't cook this up is worthless to you, I do give that assurance. The point is that even if you are ninety-nine per cent convinced that Mr. Perrit arranged for me to take this line, dare you risk that one per cent? What if I'm acting on my own hook? You would discover it too late. To me you're no asset at all unless you get money from Mr. Perrit and give most of it to me. I have no stake in you; your fate is of no concern to me. If you get money from Mr. Perrit and don't give me my share, you'll never know what minute or where you'll feel that hand on your shoulder."

"I wouldn't be there," Violet said harshly.

Wolfe sighed. "You're not thinking straight. Certainly you'd be there. You'll have to be, if you go on choosing Mr. Perrit. Incidentally, it will be useless for you to repeat this conversation to him. Naturally I have prepared for that, and he won't believe a word of it."

"The hell he won't. He told you to say it."

"No. He didn't." Wolfe pushed his chair back from the desk. "If you knew me better, Miss Murphy, you would believe me when I say that this is strictly my own idea. This is my own scheme, conceived and executed by me alone, and I expect to profit from it. So will you; I'm not trying to freeze you out. Mr. Perrit makes a lot of money. You can keep ten thousand out of every hundred thousand you get."

Wolfe arose and walked past her to the door. There he turned. "A word of caution, Miss Murphy. Your natural impulse would be to get all you can and disappear. Mr. Perrit might possibly decide not to find you, for obvious reasons. I wouldn't. I would find you. I am fully as vain as Mr. Perrit. I will not be diddled."

He went.

Violet had not turned around to see him out. She now sat with her eyes on his chair as if he were still in it. A corner of her lips was screwed around and up. She didn't seem to be in anything like a panic, merely trying to think straight. Finally she turned her eyes to me and spoke, not as to an enemy:

"My God, he's fat."

I nodded at her approvingly. "You're a brave little woman and I admire you. Luckily you don't have to toss in or boost the pot now and here. You've got time to sleep on it, which is a good idea. Shall I take you home and tuck you in?"

She smiled at me and I grinned back.

"You don't look like a grister," she said. "You look healthy and handsome."

"Inside," I said, "I am clean but mean." I stood up. "I don't offer to drive you home because I noticed you've got your own car. But I can go along just for the air."

She left her chair, crossed to me, put four fingers carefully and precisely at the top of my forehead, and ran them back over and down my scalp, giving me a comb.

"Air," she said. "Baby, do I need air!"

"We'll share it," I told her. "Ninety per cent for you and ten for me."

I got my hat and topcoat from the hall, escorted her out, opened the door of her coupé for her, and went around to the other side and climbed in. What I was actually after was not air, nor yet more hair-combing, but insurance against bodily injury. I wasn't condemning Wolfe for not informing Dazy Perrit before pulling that on her, since he might have thought it up just before she came, or even after she came, but all the same I didn't care for the sketch as it now stood. If she bounced into the penthouse and blurted it out to Perrit, which she was certainly capable of, there was no way of telling how he might react. Common sense would have told him what Wolfe was up to, trying to get nine out of ten to hand back to him, but the trouble was that there was nothing common about a bird like Perrit, not even sense. Probably he didn't think there was an honest man on earth. So there I was in her coupé with her.

She was a first-rate driver, fully half as good as me. As she slowed down for a red light at Fortieth Street I said, "Miss Murphy, you're sunk."

"Cut out the Murphy," she snapped. Then she reached to pat me on the knee. "Just call me Angel Food."

I didn't have much time, since the penthouse was on Seventy-eighth Street, not more than a few minutes away at that time of night, and I didn't really intend to go up with her and tuck her in.

"I don't like angel food," I told her. "I'll call you Maple Delight. But you're absolutely sunk if you try to bull it through. I speak frankly because I admire you in more ways than one, and also because I enjoy life and don't care to leave it at this point. If you go on putting the bee on Perrit and don't give Wolfe his nine-tenths, you're through. Wolfe is a hyena, a vulture, and a jackal. If you do give Wolfe his nine-tenths, Perrit will find it out sooner or later, and then not only will Wolfe get it, which might or might not be a calamity, but I am liable to get it too. Even if I'm not as healthy and handsome as you thought I was there for a minute, I do have my skin on straight and I like it that way."

"Go on talking." She didn't take her eyes from her driving. "You haven't said anything yet, but your voice goes through me. I won't even want a drink."

We were at Fifty-first Street. I went on, "So to show you how selfish I am, I've got a suggestion. You haven't got a chance of cleaning up, not one in a million. You're squeezed in between Dazy Perrit and Nero Wolfe, and that's no set-up for a Sherman tank, let alone a lady. The big haul is out for good, and you might as well face it and show you've got brains as well as guts."

I patted her thigh. "So take it, Maple Delight. First, you can keep the screw on Perrit, handing most of it over to Wolfe, but you'd be a sucker if you did. It wouldn't be worth your measly percentage. Second, you can slide out and away, and my opinion is no good on that because I don't know how hard you'd find it to make a living. Of course you'd have to travel, which would be a disadvantage if you like New York. Third, and this is my suggestion, you can tell Perrit—or I'll do it if you want me to—that the gyp is out, you are merely his loving and obedient daughter, but it would be nice to have the weekly handout stepped up to three centuries instead of one."

She sent me a sharp glance and back again to her driving. I somehow gathered that I was doing fine.

"Wolfe would get no cut," I said firmly. "I doubt if he would even expect it, and anyhow you can leave that to me. I have—a way of bringing pressure. Almost certainly Perrit would settle for that and no hard feelings. As for you, you don't have to be a damn pig.

That would be fifteen thousand, six hundred bucks a year, no income tax, and I suppose Perrit pays the household expenses, including such items as this car. Six hundred dollars more than a United States Senator gets! You could stay in New York, with no thought of Utah or any other desert, not to mention confined spaces, enjoy your friends, sleep as late as you want, visit the museums and art galleries—what the hell, what if two hundred is as high as he'll go? That's twice what a plumber makes! Usually I hate to be driven by a woman, but you're good. I thought you would be. You're very good."

"I can turn corners and back up," she admitted. "Yeah, art galleries. Are you comic?"

We had made it crosstown and were going north on Fifth Avenue, in the Sixties. "Someday," I said, "you must drive me up to that roadhouse Perrit owns in Westchester. I just tossed in the art galleries. Forget it. One thing, if my suggestion strikes you at all and you want to think it over, for God's sake, don't mention Wolfe's double-cross to Perrit. Not till you're sure what you want. That would start fireworks that nobody could stop."

"It would?" She was scornful. "Or it wouldn't."

"If you still think Perrit and Wolfe framed it you're batty. You don't know Wolfe."

"I know Dazy Perrit." She turned east on Seventy-eighth Street.

"But not Wolfe," I insisted. "The first chance I get I'll explain him to you. It's not only his fat that keeps you from seeing through him. Perrit has met his match twice, first you and now Wolfe."

She pulled up at the curb on the right, by an awning, and I hopped out and held the door open for her, but she emerged on her own side and came around.

She put a hand on my arm. "We'll leave the car here. Later I'll come down and drive you home."

For the second time that night I was given the job of crawling from under, and this time there was no Morton to give me an assist. I resisted, politely, the pull on my arm and started arranging words, but the words never got spoken. At that instant the question became not whether those words would get spoken, but whether

28

any more words at all would ever get spoken—by me. A car had turned into the street from Fifth Avenue, tearing along in second gear, and slowed down, nearly to a stop, just behind Violet's coupé. I was aware of it only from noises because my back was to it. When Violet's hold on my arm tightened and her face went stiff and she jerked to the left and tight against me, I reacted fast by whirling around, and the force of my whirl, with her holding my arm, yanked her to one side. The bullets were coming by then. With his gun poked through the open window, the guy in the car had a range of not more than twenty feet.

I think the first bullet got her. Anyhow, the shots came so fast together that that was a minor point. As she went down I went down with her, both because of her drag on my arm, which she held on to, and because my reflexes decided that standing up was a bad idea under the circumstances. Then other reflexes took a hand, and I rolled to the curb and was kneeling behind Violet's coupé, with the gun from my coatpocket in my hand, aiming it at the other car, which was on the move again, thirty yards toward Madison Avenue and going fast. I pulled the trigger until the gun was empty. The car was going faster as it crossed Madison.

I was upright by then and I turned to Violet. She was on her hands and knees, trying to get up. As I moved to her she crumpled. I knelt down for a look and saw that one bullet had torn through her cheek, but obviously there were others.

I told her, "Quit moving, kid. Quiet." Then I said, though you won't believe it and I find it hard to believe myself, "Angel Food."

She quit moving soon enough. "Uh—uh—" she said. She was gasping, and in between gasps sucking in breath with a hiss. She was trying to talk. "It's—uh—uh—shame," she got out. Her chin came up and she screamed at me, "Shame!" Then she gave up and flopped.

I raised up for a glance around. Windows were opening and voices came, and someone was running my way down the sidewalk from Fifth Avenue. The door of the apartment house at the other end of the awning opened, and a man in uniform came out and toward me, a doorman or elevator man. I saw that the one coming down the sidewalk was a cop, so I got upright, called out, "Doctor!" and dived into the apartment house. The lobby was empty, and so was the elevator, with its door standing open. I found the switchboard, plugged in, pushed a button, and dialed a number, trying to remember if I had left it connected to the extension in Wolfe's room, which I certainly should have done from force of habit.

I had. Finally his voice came. "Nero Wolfe speaking."

"Archie. I took her home. We were standing on the sidewalk in front of the apartment house on Seventy-eighth Street. A guy came along in a car and started shooting, and then got away. She is dead. Tell Fritz—"

"Are you hurt?"

"I'll tell the world I'm hurt, but not with bullets. That bastard Perrit decided to get her and to use us for proof of something, and you can figure out what while I spend the night as a quiz kid. Tell Fritz—"

A voice came at me from behind. "Get offa that phone! Now!"

VIII

Lieutenant Rowcliff of Homicide was one of the reasons why I doubted if the world would ever reach the point of universal brotherhood. It didn't seem feasible as long as opinions were still loose like mine of Rowcliff.

At ten minutes to three in the morning, in a torture chamber at the 19th Precinct on East Sixty-seventh Street, where he had established emergency headquarters, Rowcliff said to me, "Very well." He never used vulgar expressions like okay. "Very well, we'll lock you up."

I was yawning, and had to wait till it was finished before answering him. Then I remarked, "You've said that four times. I don't like the idea, and neither will Mr. Wolfe or his lawyer, but I prefer it to more of this. Proceed."

He merely sat and scowled at me, but no vulgar scowl, a Rowcliff scowl.

"Let me summarize it," I offered. "Dazy Perrit came to see Mr. Wolfe, to consult him. If I had information for you on that, which I haven't, it would be only secondhand. The place for you to get that is from Mr. Wolfe."

"I have told you," Rowcliff said coldly, "that I have sent a man to see Wolfe, twice, two men, and they were not allowed to enter. The door is bolted, as usual. That man Brenner talked through a crack and said that Wolfe was asleep and he wouldn't disturb him. That is the impudent and arrogant attitude to be expected."

"Try him after breakfast," I suggested. "Say, eleven o'clock." I was pleased to learn that my undelivered message to Fritz had not been necessary. "Of course I won't be there to let you in if I'm in a cell. Then, at eleven-forty, twenty minutes before midnight, Perrit's daughter arrived, apparently to consult Mr. Wolfe too. When they were through I escorted Miss Perrit home, with her driving her car. We arrived about twelve-thirty. I glanced at both my wristwatch and the dash clock at Columbus Circle, and it was twelve-twenty-six. We were standing—"

"That's all down."

"Okay, and so is this. The man in the car had a handkerchief tied—"

"How do you know it was a handkerchief?"

"Oh, my God, we're off again. Something white then, possibly torn from his shirt tail, which is why I wouldn't know him from Adam, because most of his face was behind it. I don't know whether he was after her or me or both, though I admit it was her he hit. There was a license plate on the car but I couldn't make it out, or didn't, which is unimportant since I understand it was hot, having been liberated less than a mile away an hour or so earlier. And found less than six blocks away, near the Eighty-sixth Street subway station. I would like to know if any of my bullets—"

"Where's Dazy Perrit?"

"You mean now?"

"Now."

"I have no idea."

31

"Is he holed up in Wolfe's house?"

"Good lord, no. It makes my teeth chatter just to think of it."

"Did your teeth chatter yesterday, when he was there arranging things with Wolfe?"

"Look, Lieutenant," I said grimly. "It will soon be dawn. I've told it over and over, all I know. I am now going to clam up. I knew a man once who insisted on hunting ducks with a shotgun with a recoil that knocked him flat on his prat every time he pulled the trigger. He seemed to love it. In a way you remind me of him. You know damn well the man to tell you what Perrit and his daughter wanted is Mr. Wolfe. You know damn well I can't tell you. You also know that if you hold me Mr. Wolfe will resent it and you won't be able to depend on a thing he says. What do you want to do, get in another jab in a private feud or solve a murder? I warn you I'm going to take a nap, either in a chair, on a cot, or home in bed."

"Get out of here," Rowcliff commanded. "Go on, get."

He pushed a button and passed the word, and a minute later I was on the sidewalk. What had restrained Rowcliff, I was well aware, was nothing said by me, but his uncertainty regarding the amount of co-operation his superior officer, Inspector Cramer, would be wanting from Wolfe.

Anyhow, as I voted against trying to flush a taxi and headed for the subway, it wasn't Rowcliff I was concentrating on, it was Dazy Perrit. I had come within an ace of spilling it to Rowcliff to give the cops a good start, but knew that wouldn't do before seeing Wolfe. I also, on my way home to Wolfe's house, did some useless wondering, like wondering if it was the face named Archie who had done the job.

But mostly I was trying to add it up, and couldn't even begin. The starting point was this that Perrit had decided to erase Violet without delay. That much was a cinch. But what was the big idea of dragging Wolfe in, not to mention me? How could he use the Wolfe part as a cover, either for the police or for anyone else, without letting it out that Violet was a phony? And wasn't that supposed to be the one thing he didn't want? The reason I particularly wanted those and other questions answered was because I had a certain idea. I am no one-man pestilence; the only time I have shot people it has been purely ad lib, to meet an urgent contingency; but I had decided I would have to shoot Dazy Perrit. It wasn't merely a hangover from my sensation as I had stood with Violet gripping my arm, watching that gun blaze away at us; it was a realization of where Wolfe and I were sitting and would go on sitting. The risks we took in the cases we worked on, that was all right, that was just part of it. But to be tangled up with the inside affairs of the Perrits and Meekers wasn't taking a risk, it was simply checking out, with the date of departure the only thing still to be settled.

So as I transferred to the shuttle at Grand Central I was going to shoot Perrit the first chance I got. Four minutes later, when I was transferring again at Times Square, shooting Perrit was obviously the very worst thing I could do. In another four minutes, as I emerged into Thirty-fourth Street, anything and everything was the worst thing I could do. As I felt then, the guy I really wanted to shoot was Wolfe, for having opened that window and yelled to me to bring Perrit in, in a frantic snatch at a pork chop. Turning up Ninth Avenue to Thirty-fifth and then west again, I let the brain float. I was getting close to bed and having a letdown, after all the excitement, followed by two hours of tight feelings at the precinct station with the city employees.

As I neared our stoop I changed my mind again about going to Wolfe's room for a bedside chat. It could wait till morning. I was getting some satisfaction out of that as I lifted my foot for the first step up to our door, and then instantaneously the satisfaction was gone. What chased it was two men. They came out of the dark corner behind the stone wall of the stoop, and there they were, close enough to touch.

The one on the right was the face named Archie. The one on the left, and a little back, was Dazy Perrit. The face had a gun showing, in his hand. Perrit's hands were in his coat-pockets. My guns hadn't been taken from me, since I had tickets for them, but the one in my coat-pocket wasn't loaded, and my armpit holster might as well have been up in Yonkers, since my top-coat was buttoned.

"I want to ask you about tonight," Perrit said. "My car's around the corner on Eleventh Avenue. Go ahead. We'll come behind."

"We can talk here," I told him. "I've often talked to people here." This was certainly my chance to shoot him, a perfect set-up for self-defense, but I postponed it. "What do you want to ask me?"

"Get going," he said, in a tone a little different.

It was a cockeyed situation. If I refused to budge I didn't think they would drill me, because that would have been silly. If that was what they had in mind they wouldn't have started conversing. If I went up the stoop and put the key in the door I still didn't think they would drill me, but there were two objections to it. First, they might start operations short of drilling and one thing leads to another; and, second, the door was bolted on the inside and I would have to rouse Fritz. Not to mention, third, that with Fritz roused and the door open they would probably decide to come in for a visit.

I decided to stand pat. "I like it—" I started, and stopped, hearing the sound of a car coming. I turned my head to look, because the sound of a car coming got on my nerves after my recent experience with it, and also because it might be a police car if Rowcliff had decided not to wait till eleven o'clock for another try at Wolfe. But it was only a taxicab. They often came through there late at night, on their way to the nest, a company garage around the corner.

I turned back to them. "I like it here. Even if I had ideas, which I haven't, my gun's empty, so relax. I emptied it—"

I didn't duck or dive, I just dropped, flat on the sidewalk, and started rolling. I was thinking I mustn't bang my head against the stone of the stoop. This time I didn't see the man in the taxicab at all, even enough of a glimpse to see if he had something white over his face, I was moving too fast, rolling to get around the corner. I had, as I remembered it, no sign of an impulse to reach for my gun. If I thought at all I suppose I was thinking that if a man in a taxicab want-

34

ed to make holes in Perrit and the face it was nothing to me. I had, and have, no notion what they were doing, but later examination showed that some of the noise I heard was made by them, using their own ammunition.

That noise stopped. The noise of the taxi moving from the scene tapered off. I stuck my head around the corner of the stoop, saw a form as flat at mine had been and much quieter, and scrambled to my feet. There were two forms, the other one around the other corner of the stoop, and it was twitching a little. I saw it still had a gun in its hand, so I stepped over and kicked it out and away. I knelt, first to one and then to the other, for a brief inspection, and finding it likely that no one would ever again consider it dangerous to turn his back on them, mounted the stoop to the front door and pushed the button for Fritz, my private rings. But the rings weren't needed. Before my finger left the button the door opened for the crack of two inches allowed by the chain of the bolt and a voice came through.

"Archie?"

"Me, Fritz. Open—"

"Do you need help?"

"I need help to get in. Open up."

He slid the bolt and I pushed and entered.

"Did you kill somebody?" he inquired.

Wolfe's bellow sounded from the hall one flight up. "Archie! What the devil is it now?"

His tone implied that I owed him apologies, past due, for interfering with his sleep.

"Corpses on the sidewalk in front, and it might have been me!" I called to him bitterly, and went to the office and dialed Rhinelander 4-1445, the 19th Precinct Station House.

IX

So Rowcliff didn't have to wait until eleven o'clock for a go at Wolfe, after all. Very few performances were beyond the range of Wolfe's special strain of gall, but keeping himself inaccessible with Dazy

35

Perrit and a hired man shot down in front of his house while chatting with me would really have been out of bounds.

At four-five A.M. he received Rowcliff and a sergeant in his bedroom. I missed that interview because I was occupied at the time, in the office with a committee of the squad, by request. I learned later that Wolfe had given them a peep under the lid but by no means removed it. He told them that Perrit had said he was being blackmailed by his daughter and wanted him to invent a way to make her stop, that he, Wolfe, had accepted the job, that the daughter had come to the office at Perrit's command, and that he, Wolfe, had threatened to inform the police of Salt Lake City, where she was wanted, if she didn't behave herself. The other items he kept, such as Violet being a phony and the kind of lever she was using to heist her father. He left Beulah out entirely. I learned this later, and didn't know then how far he was going, so down in the office with the committee I backed away from everything but the outdoor facts, adding nothing to my popularity but not really endangering my health.

The understanding had been that a specified number could enter for conversation with Wolfe and me, but that the house was not to be used for a command post, so the turmoil out front, complete with spotlights, was not allowed to spill over the sill, and Fritz was standing by. I was taken out twice, first to go all over it on the spot, and the second time to try to catch me in contradictions, but no one ever even suggested that I should go for a ride. From the way they acted it wasn't hard to tell why: they were sorry for me. I hadn't had time to analyze the situation enough to realize how awful right they were.

That went on long after daylight was showing, until the sun was entering at the window beyond Wolfe's desk. As soon as they were all gone, including Rowcliff and the sergeant from Wolfe's room, Fritz went to the kitchen and started breakfast. I mounted one flight, knocked on the door, was told to enter, and did so. Wolfe, in yellow silk pajamas and yellow slippers with turned-up toes, was coming out of the bathroom.

"Well, " I began, "I hope to God—"

The phone rang. Whenever I left the office I plugged in extensions. Wolfe's instrument, on his bedside table, was bright yellow and I didn't like it. I crossed over and got it and told the transmitter, "Nero Wolfe's office."

"Archie? Saul. I want the boss."

I told Wolfe, "Saul Panzer."

He nodded, approaching. "Good. Go up to your room and look at your face. It needs washing."

"So would yours if you had spent the night rolling around on sidewalks. You mean you have private business with Saul? Have you got him working on something?"

"Certainly. Mr. Perrit's job."

"Since when?"

"I phoned him last evening while you were taking Miss Page home. Go and wash your face."

I went. Usually I resented it when Wolfe froze me out of operations with one of the men he used, but now I was too played out to bother, and besides, Saul was different. It was hard to resent anything about a guy as good as Saul Panzer. At the mirror in my bathroom I saw that there was no question about my face, so I attended to it, deciding to postpone shaving until after breakfast, and then went back down one flight to Wolfe's room. He had finished his private talk with Saul and was sitting in his underwear, putting on his socks.

"What do you want to discuss?" I asked him.

"Nothing."

I stared indignantly. "Well, by God."

He grunted. "At the moment there is nothing to discuss. You're out of it. I told Mr. Rowcliff that I engaged to make Mr. Perrit's daughter stop blackmailing him, and that I threatened her with exposure to the police, and that's all. He's an imbecile. He intimated that I am liable to prosecution for attempting to blackmail the daughter." Wolfe straightened up. "By the way, I suppose it would be futile to call that number, Lincoln six-three two three two, now that Mr. Perrit is dead?"

"I'm out of it," I said through my teeth and went down to the kitchen for breakfast. Out of it! Look who was calling Rowcliff an imbecile! I even forgot to taste the first three pancakes as they went down.

My breakfast was interrupted four times by phone calls. Of course that would go on all day. Only one of the four, the last one, required reporting to Wofe, which suited me fine, since I wished to keep communication with him at the lowest possible minimum. By that time he had finished breakfast and gone up to the plant room, so I gave him a buzz on the house phone.

"A man called," I told him, "and said his name is L. A. Schwartz and he's Dazy Peritt's lawyer. He wanted to come to see you immediately. I told him eleven o'clock. I have his number. If you regard him as out of it too, I can ring him and tell him not to come."

"Eleven will do," Wolfe said. "Did you try that Lincoln number? Mr. Perrit said between seven and ten."

"No," I said and hung up.

For the next hour and three-quarters my main job would have been to stay awake if it hadn't been for the phone. Stalling journalists had got to be routine with me over the years, but it took time to handle it so they wouldn't get down on us. One of the calls was a sample of what might be expected from life from then on as long as it lasted. A guy with a hoarse voice, so hoarse I wished he would take time out to clear his throat, said he was a friend of Dazy Perrit's and he would like to ask me a couple of questions, and would I meet him at the Seven-Eleven Club some time that afternoon? I told him I was tied up at the office but if he would give me his name and number I would ring him if I found I could make it. He said he didn't know where he would be, so skip it and he would try again. Then he said, "It was too bad you wasn't tied up at the office last night," and hung up.

Another call came from Saul Panzer just before eleven. I put it through to Wolfe and was instructed to stay off the line, an instruction I didn't need since I was out of it. Before they were through talking the doorbell rang again, for about the tenth time since the cops had left, and this time it was not a gate-crasher to be shooed off but a customer with a reserved seat. I allowed L. A. Schwartz to enter, told him Wolfe would

38

soon appear, and herded him to the office and to a chair.

I wouldn't have picked him for Dazy Perrit's lawyer. For one thing, he wore old-fashioned nose-pinchers for glasses, which didn't seem to be the thing. He was sixty, skinny, and silent. I thought I might keep myself awake another five minutes by striking up a conversation, but I got a total of not more than ten words out of him. He sat with his brief case on his lap and every thirty seconds pulled at the lobe of his right ear. I had abandoned him by the time the sound of Wolfe's elevator came.

On his way across to his desk Wolfe halted to acknowledge the introduction, made by me in spite of being out of it, purely for the sake of appearances. Then he went to his chair, sat and got himself adjusted, leaned back, and took in the visitor with half-closed eyes.

"Well, sir?" he asked.

Schwartz blinked against the light from the window. "I must apologize," he said, "for being urgent about this appointment, but I felt there should be no delay." He sounded formal.. "I gathered from Mr. Perrit last evening that you had not explicitly given your assent, and therefore—"

"May I ask, assent to what?"

"To your appointment, in his will, as executor of his estate and in effect the guardian of his daughter. Did you?"

"Utterly"—Wolfe wiggled a finger at him—"preposterous."

"I was afraid of that," Schwartz said regretfully. "It will complicate matters. I'm afraid it's partly my fault, drafting the documents in such haste. There is a question whether the fifty thousand dollars provided for that purpose will go to the executor if the executor is not you but someone appointed by a court."

Wolfe grunted. His eyes opened and then half closed again. "Tell me about it," he said.

Schwartz opened the flap of his brief case, then let it drop back again, and kept it on his lap.

"In the past," he said, "I have attended to a few little matters for Mr. Perrit of a purely legal nature. I know law, but on account of my temperament I am not a successful lawyer. Last evening he came to my home—a modest little apartment on Perry Street—he has never been to my office—and asked me to draw up some papers at once, in his presence. Luckily I have a typewriter at home but it isn't very good and you'll have to overlook typographical deficiencies. It took a long while because of the special conditions to be covered. It's a difficult business, extremely difficult, to convey property by testament to a daughter without naming her and indeed without identifying her in any way."

The lawyer blinked. "I should tell you right off that there will be no problems of administration. The property consists exclusively of government bonds and cash in banks, a little over a million dollars. In that respect there are no intricacies. All other property owned by Mr. Perrit, including his interest in various enterprises, goes to others—his associates—in another document. Your functions are limited strictly to the legacy to his daughter. There are only two other provisions in the document under consideration: fifty thousand dollars to you as executor, and the same amount to me. The witnesses to it were a man who owns a delicatessen and a young woman who runs a rental library, both of whom are known to me. I have the original in my possession. Mr. Perrit took a copy."

Wolfe lifted a hand. "Let me see it."

Schwartz blinked again. "In a moment, yes, sir. I should explain that the large sum left to me was not to compensate me for drawing up some papers. It was Mr. Perrit's way of insuring my performance of an act mentioned nowhere in writing, but only orally. I drafted another document of which no copy was made. It was put into an envelope along with other sheets of paper on which Mr. Perrit had written something, I don't know what, and the envelope was sealed with wax. I was given the function and the responsibility, in the event of Mr. Perrit's death, of delivering the envelope to you personally at the earliest possible moment, together with the information, already delivered, regarding the will. I would put it this way: of the fifty thousand dollars left to me, one hundred dollars was for drafting the documents, another hundred was for making the delivery to you—reasonable sums—and the remainder was to pay me for not opening the envelope and examining the contents. He misjudged me entirely. One-tenth that amount, even one-fiftieth, would have been enough."

He opened his brief case, took out folded papers, and put them on Wolfe's desk. "That's the will, which I must take with me for probate." He produced a bulky envelope with red blotches of wax and put it beside the papers. "That's the envelope."

He sat back and pulled at his ear.

Wolfe reached for the envelope and papers. First he went through the will, thoroughly—he is never a fast reader—then handed it to me and slit the envelope with his paper knife. As he finished with a page of the contents of the envelope he slid it across to my reach; apparently I was back in again. I read faster than he does, so I was only a couple of minutes behind him at the end.

The will was certainly involved. It was hard for me to tell whether the cash and bonds were left to Nero Wolfe or to the unnamed and unidentified "my daughter," but I'm not a lawyer and I suppose it was legally hers, though it seemed to me to leave room for a lot of antics by him if his mind worked that way. The other document drawn up by Schwartz, the one in the envelope, was very technical. It contained a long list of bonds and balances in banks, and its chief purpose seemed to be to make them available to Wolfe if, as, and when he felt like taking them over. In places it sounded like a power of attorney, and in other places like blessings and absolution for Wolfe no matter what he did. If Dazy Perrit had sat around while Schwartz composed all that and typed it out, one of the problems the police were working on—how and where Perrit had spent the hours preceding his death—was certainly solved.

But he hadn't merely sat. He had done some composing too, namely, the papers he had written on himself and put in the envelope. I read that last and slowest. It began:

> *391 Perry St,*
> *N.Y. City,*
> *Oct. 7,*
> *1946,*
> *9.42 Pm.*

Mr. Nero Wolfe, Esq.
909 W. 35 St, N.Y. City,
Dear sir, If this is a wrong one I'm pulling its the worst mistake I ever made but I think I can count on you after seeing you today and sizing you up. I don't think I'm going to die but what if I do thats my problem my daughter has got to be protected I mean she has got to get what belongs to her and thats my problem.

There was a line and a half crossed out and then he went on. I have it in front of me now, but it covers seven pages and what the hell. All it amounted to was this, that the fifty thousand bucks was to pay Wolfe for seeing that Beulah got the cash and bonds, for keeping it all under his hat, and for using his best judgment as to how much Beulah should ever be told, and, if so, when. Then there were a lot of facts, about who the mother was and so on, and dates, and the last two pages might have been classed as philosophy. Dazy Perrit's philosophy. The two other papers in the envelope were a marriage certificate, dated St. Louis, September 4, 1924, and a birth certificate, dated July 26, 1925.

I folded things up again and stuck them in the envelope.

"Put it in the safe," Wolfe said.

I did so.

Schwartz quit pulling at his ear and began talking. "There might be some reluctance about handling money accumulated by the methods used by Mr. Perrit.

42

But it would be a great responsibility to deprive a young woman—"

He stopped because Wolfe was waving it away with a finger. "Bah," Wolfe said. "If an oil marauder or a steel bandit gets respect for his wishes regarding the disposal of his loot, why shouldn't Mr. Perrit?"

"Then you accept the—ah—office?"

"I do."

Instead of looking relieved and satisfied, the lawyer frowned. "In that case, I have a question. With the daughter dead, how do you propose to perform the functions of your office?"

"That, sir, is my affair. I don't—" Wolfe stopped himself, cocking an eye. "No. I'm wrong. Since Mr. Perrit trusted you he would expect me to give you this much satisfaction: the daughter is not dead. Beyond that Mr. Perrit left it to me, and so will you."

"I see." Schwartz blinked. "I hope you'll forgive me if I mention another detail. My personal interest is concerned, because fifty thousand dollars is for me an extremely large sum, and if I don't get it through you I may not get at all. I understand that your assistant—this gentleman here—was present when Miss Perrit was killed, and was also present when Mr. Perrit and his companion were killed, and that he, your assistant, was not injured. I do not know whether you fully realize the inferences that will be drawn and the consequences that may reasonably be expected. Those inferences will be greatly strengthened when this will—" he tapped a finger on his brief case, to which the will had been returned—"is probated and becomes public knowledge, as the law requires. With over a million dollars entrusted to your hands and you accountable to no one. Mr. Perrit's associates will inevitably draw those inferences, which will seem obvious to them, and they—"

The phone rang, and I took it. It was the hoarse man who had previously invited me to meet him at the Seven-Eleven Club, and he still hadn't found time to clear his throat. This time he wanted Wolfe, and Wolfe, after I had covered the transmitter and told him about the previous call, got on. I stayed on too, as I always do when not told to get off, but I'll only report one end.

43

"Nero Wolfe speaking. ... Your name, please? ... I'm sorry, sir, I never speak to people without a name; I must have your name. ... F-A-B-I-A-N? ... Thank you. Hold the line a moment, please."

Wolfe asked Schwartz, "Have you ever heard of a man named Fabian?"

"Yes." Schwartz was frowning and all his fingers were gripping the edge of his brief case.

"So have I," I said emphatically.

"Yes, Mr. Fabian, what is it? ... I see. I never make appointments outside my house. ... No, no indeed, I assure you I'm not frightened at all. ... Yes, I realize that, but I seldom go out. ... Well, I have a suggestion. Why don't you come to my office, say at two o'clock today? ... Good. ... That's right. You have the address? ... Good."

He hung up. I did likewise, with a vicious bang.

Schwartz said, in a different tone from any he had used, "I was about to say when the phone rang that Mr. Perrit's associates are men of action. To put it baldly, they will kill both you and your assistant the first chance they get. I was about to suggest certain precautions. Frankly, as I said, my personal interest is concerned. The best way—"

"Mr. Fabian says he wants to ask me something."

"But great heavens!" Schwartz was looking green. "He's the most notorious—to invite him—to let him in—"

"If he is really dangerous," Wolfe said stiffly, "and if he has drawn the sort of inferences you fear, my own office is the only safe place to meet him. This business has to be settled sooner—"

The phone rang again. I reached for it, told it, "Nero Wolfe's office, Archie Goodwin speaking," and got a shock in my ear in the shape of an agitated voice declaring loud enough to be heard out in the kitchen, "You said your name was Harold Stevens!"

I said sharply, "Hold it a second. Stay on," and turned to Wolfe and told him in a bored tone, "It's the friend of that law student. May go on for an hour. Shall I go upstairs and take it?"

"Yes. We might as well get it over with. She can come any time. Arrange it properly."

44

I never bothered with the elevator, and anyhow, up three steps at a time was quicker. Up in my room, with the door shut, I didn't take time to make myself comfortable in a chair, but grabbed the phone and told it, "Sorry to keep you waiting, but there were people around and I came upstairs. What's the trouble?"

"You said your name was Stevens!"

"Yeah. Of all the millions of details in the world, one of the most unimportant right now is my name. My name is mud. Stevens or Goodwin, mud."

"It's important to me."

"Thank you very much. It that what you called to say?"

"No, it isn't. I want to know about the man that got killed and how you happened—"

"Wait a minute. Collect yourself and start at the beginning. What have you seen, heard, and done?"

"I've seen pictures, just now in the *Gazette*. One is of a man named Dazy Perrit, and I know him—I don't really know him well, but I know him in a certain way, and he has been killed, and for a certain reason that's bad news for me. Another picture is of you, it's a very good likeness, and it says your name is Archie Goodwin and you work for Nero Wolfe—it calls you his legman—and it says you were with Dazy Perrit when he was killed. So I want to know—"

"Excuse me," I cut her off, "but the kind of things you want to know are not a good kind for a telephone. I would like to come up there for a talk but I have things to do. Why don't you hop on the subway and come down here? Will you do that?"

"I certainly will! I will be there—"

"Excuse me again. The sidewalk in front of our house is the scene of two murders and therefore temporarily conspicuous. Get this. From Thirty-fourth Street and Eleventh Avenue go east on Thirty-fourth Street. It's ninety-two paces for me, so it will be about a hundred and twenty for you. At that point there is a narrow passage between two buildings—a loading platform on the left of it and a wholesale paper products place on the right. Go in along the passageway and I'll meet you at the far end of it and let you in at our back door. Have you got it?"

45

"Certainly. It ought to take me about half an hour."

"Okay. I'll be there, but if I'm not, wait for me."

"All right. Tell me just one thing, was Dazy Perrit's daughter—"

I told her nothing doing and ended it. A glance at my wristwatch, on the fly as I headed for the stairs, showed me eleven-fifty-two. At the bottom I slowed to a normal pace, to enter the office with an attitude of indifference, but that proved unnecessary because L. A. Schwartz was gone. Wolfe sat at his desk pouring beer.

"She saw pictures of Perrit and me in the *Gazette*," I reported. "She'll come the back way and be here in half an hour."

"Satisfactory." He put the bottle down. "Take her straight upstairs to the south room. She must be seen by no one." He scowled at me. "Confound it, I suppose she must be invited to lunch. Sit down and tell me everything that happened last night."

"I thought I was out of it. When did I get in again?"

"Pfui. Go ahead."

Having been reporting uncombed events to Wolfe for over ten years, I had got expert at it, but this called for extra concentration since the time was limited. I tried to get it all in and make a clean job of it, but he had questions to put as usual, and was still asking them when the clock said twelve-twenty and I had to go. I left by way of the kitchen and the back stairs, emerging into our little private yard where Fritz grows chives and tarragon and other vegetation. Leaving the door through the solid board fence unlocked, since it wouldn't get out of my sight, I skirted piles of rubbish on the premises south of us, and another twenty steps got me to the entrance of the passage. There was no one there. But I didn't wait long. Within a couple of minutes a figure appeared at the other end of the passage, looked in, and started toward me. Only it wasn't Beulah. It was the law student. She was right behind him, and as they approached me she darted around to the front and spoke first.

"It's all right that Morton came along, isn't it? He wouldn't let me come alone."

"Well, he's here," I growled. "Hello." My impulse was to tell him to go home and study, because we already had complications enough, but since we had made him so welcome the night before, and him practically a member of the family, I decided not to make an issue of it.

"Watch where you step," I told them and led the way back around the rubbish piles, through the door in the fence, which I locked, into the basement, up to the kitchen, and on up two more flights to the south room, which was on the same floor as mine, at the other end of the hall. It wasn't often used, but was by no means wasted space. On various occasions all kinds had slept in it, from a Secretary of State to a woman who had poisoned three husbands and was making a fourth one very sick.

Wolfe was there, standing by a window. There was no chair in that room that would take him without complaints from both him and the chair. He did his little bow, head forward eleven-sixteenths of an inch.

"How do you do, Miss Page. And Morton. You came along?"

"Yes, sir." Morton was firm. "I would like to know what this is all about. Goodwin saying his name was Stevens—"

"Of course. Not illegal, no felony, but at least odd. Miss Page deserves an explanation, and she'll get it. Doubtless you'll get it too, later, from her. Mr. Goodwin and I are taking Miss Page up to the plant rooms to show her my orchids and have a talk with her." He waved a hand. "There are books and magazines here, or you may go down to the office if you prefer."

The muscles of Morton's jaw had set. "I must insist—"

"No. Don't try." Wolfe was curt. "Since this concerns Miss Page, I do not intend to substitute my discretion for hers. We'll rejoin you in half an hour or so. Archie, tell Fritz that there will be two luncheon guests, at one sharp."

XI

Wolfe never tries to deny he's vain, but I doubt if he'll ever admit that it's an exercise of vanity when he takes someone who is under a strain up to the plant rooms. He acts nonchalant, but I can tell when he's enjoying himself. Beulah met expectations. In the blaze of the Cattleya room she only looked dazed, but the Dendrobiums and Phalaenopsis really got her. She stopped dead and just looked, with her mouth open.

"Someday," Wolfe said, not sounding pleased, with his usual self-control, "you must spend an hour up here. Or two hours. Now I'm afraid we haven't time."

He nudged her along to the potting room and told Theodore, the orchid nurse, that he had better go and see to the ventilators. When Theodore had gone and Wolfe was in his chair and Beulah and I on stools, he said abruptly, "You're not an infant, Miss Page. You're nineteen years old."

She nodded. "In Georgia I could vote."

"So you could. Then I won't have to use a nipple for this. We'll ignore non-essentials; they can be dealt with later, at more leisure—as, for instance, why Mr. Goodwin chose such a name as Harold Stevens to lure you down here yesterday. Do you know what a hypothetical question is?"

"Certainly."

"Then I'll put one to you. Suppose these things: that with me as intermediary, your father has arranged to make available to you a considerable sum of money; that he is not in a position to disclose himself to you and cannot ever be expected to do so; that he has put it wholly within my discretion whether you shall be told his name and your mother's name; and that the circumstances are such that it will be a deuce of a job to keep you from guessing his name and guessing it right. Supposing all that, here's something for you to think over."

Wolfe pointed a finger at her. "Do you want me to tell you the names or not?"

"I don't need to think it over. I want you to tell me."

"That's an impulse."

"It is not an impulse. Good lord, an impulse? If you only knew what I—for years—" Beulah made a little gesture. "I want to know."

"What if your father is—say, a convicted pickpocket?"

"I don't care what he is! I want to know!"

48

"Then you should. Mr. Perrit, your father, died last night." Wolfe inclined his head toward a window. "Out there on the saidewalk."

"I knew it," Beulah said calmly.

"The devil you did!"

But she wasn't actually as calm as she sounded. Her hands were clasped tight together and she had started a swallowing marathon. She didn't even try to resume the conversation, but just sat, and all signs indicated the same outcome. The outcome arrived in something like a minute. It started with her shoulders going up and down in a minor convulsion, and then her head went forward and her hands went up to cover her face, and the regulation sounds began to come.

"Good God," Wolfe muttered in a tone of horror, and got to his feet and went. In a moment, above the sounds Beulah was making, I heard the bang of his elevator door. I merely sat and waited, thinking it was natural for me to understand better than he did the most desirable and effective course of action when a young woman began to cry. After all, I thought, I see a good deal more of them than he does.

Time passed by. I was deciding the moment had come for a sympathetic hand on her shoulder when her face came up and she blurted, "Why haven't you got sense enough to go too?"

It didn't faze me. "I have," I said politely, "but I was waiting for the noise to die down enough for you to hear me tell you that if you don't want to go in the room where Morton is in your present condition, the room at the front on that floor is mine, is unlocked, and has a bathroom with a mirror."

I left her alone with it. On the way out I warned Theodore what was going on in the potting room and advised him to find jobs elsewhere. On my floor I stopped in my room to make sure about clean towels in the bathroom and general appearances. As I returned to the hall the door of the south room opened and Morton was there.

"Where's Miss Page?" he demanded. "What's going on?"

"She's up looking at orchids," I told him en route. "Relax. Lunch in ten minutes."

Down in the office Wolfe was sitting at his desk, looking harassed.

I crossed to mine, sat, and told him, "They want a shoulder to cry on, but with her fiancé under the same roof I didn't think it would be fitting. Morton is pacing—"

The phone rang. I answered it, and heard a voice I had been expecting to hear all day. I told Wolfe Inspector Cramer would like to speak to him. He got on and I stayed on.

"Nero Wolfe speaking, Mr. Cramer. How are you?"

"I'm fine. You?"

"The way I always am just before lunch. Hungry."

"Well, enjoy it. This is just a friendly call. I wanted to let you know you were right as usual when you decided to keep it all to yourself and tell Rowcliff only one thing that was worth a damn, about Perrit's daughter being wanted in Salt Lake. We got onto her through the Washington fingerprint files, as you knew we would. I don't think she was his daughter at all. Her name was Angelina Murphy, though of course she used others. She had about ten years coming. I just wanted to tell you that, but I suppose I might as well ask if you have anything to add."

"No—no, I think not."

"Nothing at all? About the job you took on for Perrit?"

"Nothing."

"Okay, I didn't expect it. Enjoy your lunch."

I pushed the phone back. I turned to Wolfe and spoke with feeling. "At least I heard that before I died. Cramer knowing you've got things he could use and merely telling you to enjoy your lunch! No pressure, no hard words, nothing! Not even bothering to drop in on us! And you know why? He's religious and he thinks it would be out of place! He thinks the only guy that belongs here now is a priest for the last rites!"

"Quite right," Wolfe agreed. "It was in effect an obituary. If I were a sentimentalist I would be touched. Mr. Cramer has never before shown the slightest interest in my enjoyment of a meal. He thinks I haven't long to live."

"Including me."

"Yes, you too, of course."

"And what do you think?"

"I haven't given it—"

The phone rang again. With a suspicion that it was Cramer, who had decided he had been too sentimental, I got it and spoke. The voice was as familiar as Cramer's but it wasn't his. "Saul Panzer," I told Wolfe, and, since he didn't give me the sign to keep off, I kept on. But it was brief and didn't fill in any gaps for me.

"Saul?"

"Yes, sir."

"Have you had lunch?"

"No, sir."

"How soon can you get here?"

"Eight to ten minutes."

"There is a change or two in the program, dictated by circumstances. I'll need you here earlier than I thought. Come and join us at luncheon—Miss Beulah Page, Mr. Morton Schane, Archie, and me."

"Yes, sir. Probably eight minutes."

XII

Whether Wolfe enjoyed his lunch or not, I didn't.

It is my habit to make big discounts anyhow, and that day I reached my all-time peak in skepticism. I didn't think he had any program whatever. I thought his line that he needed Saul, and he knew what for, was unadulterated guff. I was sure that Cramer had laid off because he had all the stuff he wanted, through the flock of stools the police always know where to find, and he regarded Wolfe and me as bad company even for an inspector. I thought the only reason Wolfe asked Saul to lunch was to have someone to talk to about something pleasant.

The last thought proved to be sound. It was not a meal full of sparkle. Morton was aloof and not a bit intimate. Beulah, who showed no traces of the recent irrigation, was trying to pretend she wasn't somewhere else, without great success. I was so firmly convinced that it was a hell of a time for a man to sit and eat that I had to grit my teeth to stay in my chair, and

51

you can neither chew nor talk very well with your teeth gritted. So the conversation was almost exclusively confined to Wolfe and Saul. Saul, in a suit that didn't fit, and needing a shave as usual, could do almost anything better than anyone I knew—even talk. They discussed plant germination, the meat shortage, books about Roosevelt, and the World Series.

At one-fifty-five Wolfe pushed his chair back and said he was sorry to end the meal so abruptly but callers were expected. He thought it best for Beulah and Morton to leave the way they had come.

Beulah protested that she wasn't going to leave, that there were things she wanted to ask about. She would wait until the callers had gone. Then, Wolfe said, she could go back to the plant rooms and do her waiting there, and also Morton if he wished to stay.

"We'll do that," Beulah agreed. She was out of her chair and moving to the dining-room door. "Come on, Morton."

But the law student balked. The way the light was I could see his eyes behind his black-rimmed glasses, and they looked determined. His voice matched them. "I don't like the way things look here. I don't know what explanation you have given Miss Page about last night. Then what happened in front of this house afterwards. And asking Miss Page to sneak in the back way. Who are these callers you're expecting?"

To my surprise, Wolfe obliged him. "One of them," he said, "is a man named Fabian. The other is named Schwartz. L. A. Schwartz, a lawyer. A member of the bar."

That was news to me. He must have invited Schwartz after I left the office.

"Are they connected with this—with Miss Page's affairs?" Morton demanded.

"With Miss Page, no. With her affairs, yes."

"I want to see them. I intend to be present."

Beulah didn't approve and said so. Wolfe said that her name would not appear in the conversation and that there was no reason why Morton shouldn't be there if he wanted to. That settled it. The fiancée started upstairs for the plant rooms, and the fiancé went with the rest of us to the office. As we were crossing the hall the doorbell rang, and I went to answer it.

Fingering back the edge of the curtain over the glass panel for a look through, and seeing it was Schwartz, I opened up. He had his brief case and was wearing the same suit and nose-pinchers, but in spite of that he was a different man. In the morning his face had been pale and colorless; now it was rosy. Before I hadn't smelled him at all; now I couldn't help smelling him. He had been spending some of the fifty grand in advance, at the courage counter. Judging from the smell, he had alternated with gin, rum, rye, vodka, and turpentine. My study of him was cut short because the bell rang again as I was hanging up his coat, and this time it was an object deserving much closer and longer study.

It was Fabian.

I had seen him around, at the ringside at fights and so on, but never met him. I had never had any desire to meet him. The most famous fact about his physical make-up, that he had no nose, wasn't true. His nose was almost normal in size and shape when you looked at it, but the point was that three other features—the mouth, ears, and eyes—grabbed the scene and the nose might as well not have been there.

Schwartz was still there, standing rigid by the coat rack, clasping his brief case. I began politely, "Do you two gentlemen—"

"You're Schwartz," Fabian stated, hoarse as ever.

"Yes, Mr. Fabian," the lawyer said hastily. He wasn't too plastered to talk straight. "You may remember—"

"Yeah." Fabian's head jerked to me. "Which way?"

I took a step, but checked it because the door between the hall and the front room opened and Wolfe appeared. He said, in his best manner, "Good afternoon, Mr. Schwartz. If you'll go to the office and make yourself comfortable we'll join you shortly." He paused. Schwartz, getting the cue, marched down the hall toward the door to the office. Wolfe turned. "Mr. Fabian? How do you do, sir? I'm Nero Wolfe." He had a hand out, and Fabian came through for a shake. Wolfe was going on, "Would you step in here for a private word with me?" He moved toward the door to the front room.

Fabian, not budging, looked at me, which struck me as childish under the circumstances, but not caring to make a point of it I followed Wolfe, and Fabian followed me. When he had passed through I closed the door, and saw at a glance that the connecting door to the office was already shut. They were both soundproofed.

Figured by pounds, Wolfe would have made more than two of Fabian. Figured by survival potential, it was anybody's guess. Wolfe didn't seem to be concerned with either calculation. He only said, "It is a part of your legend, sir, that you never go anywhere unarmed. Are you armed now?"

As far as I could see there wasn't the slightest change in the expression of Fabian's eyes, but a little crease showed between his eyebrows, as if he wasn't sure he had heard right. Then apparently he decided he had, because the crease disappeared.

"Yeah," he said. "Any objections?"

"None at all. But—I'm not calling you a liar—but I would be better satisfied if I saw proof. Where is your weapon? Easily available?"

"Yeah."

"Would you mind showing it to me?"

"Comedy," Fabian said. The crease had appeared again. "I could have had it out and in again twenty times. I came to get some proof from you. You and this Goodwin—"

"Excuse me." Wolfe was crisp and cool. "We'll go in the office and sit down. The people in there are a lawyer, Mr. Schwartz, a law student, Mr. Schane, and a man who works for me, Mr. Panzer." He had stepped to the connecting door and was opening it. "This way, sir."

I followed him, preceding Fabian in accordance with the underworld's Emily Post. Wolfe stood in the middle of the office and pronounced names, but there was no handshaking. Fabian got the scene with a slow take, his head doing the arc from right to left, and then picked a chair backed up against a section of the bookshelves. Schwartz was in the red leather chair, and Morton

Schane was off to my right, on the couch in the corner made by the wall of the lavatory that had been built in. Saul Panzer, in a chair with its back to the wall, was six feet the other side of Schwartz.

Wolfe, from behind his desk, looked around at us, then leveled off at Fabian. He spoke casually. "I must apologize, sir, for appropriating a few moments of your time. I realize it is your time, since you made an appointment to come here, and therefore you should have first say. But this will only take me—"

The damn doorbell rang. Wolfe went right on, but darted a glance at me when he saw I was staying put. I met the glance deadpan. Without consulting him about it, I had told Fritz to attend to the door if the bell rang, not intending to do any trotting in and out under the circumstances. I suppose I should have told him to keep the door bolted, which he never did when I was there unless so instructed, but subconsciously I must have figured that with Fabian already inside it wouldn't matter who else came. The result was that unwelcome noises came from the hall, including voices, one of which was Fritz's yelling for me.

"Archie! ARCHIE!"

I was up and on my way, but the gate-crasher must have galloped right through Fritz, for I was still ten feet short of the door to the hall when he entered the office. At sight of him I locked my brakes and held my breath. What was flashing through my mind was nothing you could call a thought, but just a pair of facts. One was Fabian. The other was Thumbs Meeker. I backed up so fast I bumped into the corner of Wolfe's desk, and hung there, looking. Fabian was on his feet and was furnishing the proof Wolfe had asked for. It was in his hand, with his elbow against his hip and his forearm extended. Schwartz had left the red leather chair and was kneeling on the floor behind it.

As far as Meeker and Fabian were concerned, they were the only two there. Their gazes had met and held. Fabian's gun was steady and pointed, the same as his eyes, but no blast came. Meeker's hands hung at his sides.

"You'd better lift 'em," Fabian said, no less hoarse and no more. Besides having his gun out, he also had

55

the best of it in size of target, since Meeker was well over six feet and weighed a good two-twenty.

"Not here and now," Meeker said in a thin voice.

"Who gave you the steer?"

"Nobody. I came on business."

"Lift 'em up."

"Tommyrot!" Wolfe blurted at them, but none of their four eyes moved. He went on, "This is preposterous! Besides you two, there are five people here. If you shoot him, Mr. Fabian, what do you expect to do, shoot all of us? Nonsense. The same consideration holds for the other gentleman." He addressed the other gentleman. "Who the devil are you, sir? What do you mean, bounding into my house like this?"

That relaxed me. I thought to myself, okay, say it ends—today, tomorrow. Before I die at least I get this. Before I die I get to hear Wolfe bawling hell out of Thumbs Meeker for dashing in to where Fabian is ready with his gun out. I felt I owed them something. So I said, "That's Mr. Meeker, Mr. Wolfe. Mr. Meeker, this is Nero Wolfe."

"You heard me," Meeker said in his thin voice. "Not here and now. He's right. I came here on business."

Fabian didn't say anything. His arm didn't straighten out, but his hand receded until it was where his elbow had been, and both hand and gun slid into his side coat-pocket and stayed there.

Wolfe demanded, "You came here on business? What business?"

Meeker turned, letting his eyes leave Fabian. They aimed at Wolfe. "Who are these guys?"

"They're here on business too. What is yours?"

"By God." Meeker smiled. That smile was famous, and I decided it justified its reputation. "I don't know if I care to make it public. With Fabian here. He might think I was backing out, and I don't back out." He turned again, not fast. "I don't back out, Fabian."

Fabian had nothing to say. He was still standing up.

"Confound it," Wolfe said testily. "What do you want?"

Meeker turned again, and smiled again. "I want to know if it's true that you told the cops that your punk put a finger on Perrit and his daughter for me."

56

"No."

"They seem to have that idea."

"That isn't true."

Meeker's smile came again. It came and went. "Oh," he said. "I'm a liar."

"I don't know whether you're a liar or not. But if the police have made any such statement of intimation, they are. I would have expected you to be sufficiently familiar with police methods not to come running to me with anything as silly as that."

"You didn't tell them that?"

"Certainly not."

Meeker looked at me. I was back at my desk. "You're Goodwin. Did you?"

"No," I said. "Am I a half-wit?"

"Mr. Meeker." Wolfe was curt. "Now that you're here, I suggest that you stay. Be seated. You'll be interested in what I have to say. When you entered I was about to tell these people who killed Mr. Perrit and his daughter and how and why. It will be doubly interesting because the man who did it is present."

You could have heard a cockroach stomping. Schwartz, who was back in the red leather chair, was blinking as if he would never stop again. Morton was sitting on the edge of the couch, his palms on his knees. Saul Panzer hadn't moved as much as a finger since Wolfe and I had brought Fabian in.

Fabian, still on his feet, rasped. "I don't want to miss that."

"I'm present," Meeker said.

"Yes, sir, but it wasn't you. Sit down. I don't like to talk to faces on different levels. You too, Mr. Fabian."

I then saw Thumbs Meeker being self-conscious. There were three vacant chairs, not counting Fabian's. He glanced around at them, hesitating, wanting a good tactical position, got conscious that we were all watching, didn't like that, and dropped himself onto the closest one, which put him with his back to Fabian. With that settled, Fabian sat down too, but his hand didn't come out of his pocket.

Wolfe leaned back and his fingertips met at the summit of his magnificent middle. "First," he said, "about Mr. Perrit's daughter. The people know that the young woman who was killed last night was not his daughter, but they do not know that he actually has a daughter. I do, and I know who and where she is, because Mr. Perrit told me about her in this room yesterday. At this moment she is—"

"Go slow," Fabian said. I never heard him speak without wishing to God he would clear his throat.

"If you please," Wolfe snapped. "No power on earth, Mr. Fabian, not even the kind of primitive power you rely on will keep me from telling this properly. You could shoot me, but you're not going to, so don't interrupt. Mr. Perrit's daughter is at this moment in this house, upstairs looking at my orchids. He—"

"That's a lie!" Morton Schane declared, with his chin jerked up.

"She doesn't think so." Wolfe's eyes went to him. "Stop interrupting me. Mr. Perrit entrusted her interests to me, and I intend to guard them. I'm not going to waste time telling you men things you already know. You know he had a daughter and was keeping her identity concealed, both from his enemies and from his friends. Some eighteen months ago he discovered that Mr. Meeker had learned of her existence and was trying to find her, so he tried a finesse. He went to Salt Lake City and arranged with a young woman named Murphy, a fugitive from justice, to come to New York and live with him as his daughter."

"Go slow," Fabian said.

"Don't be absurd, Mr. Fabian. The police know all that. The arrangement was made, and Miss Murphy came to New York and became Miss Violet Perrit. But before long she violated the agreement. She began demanding sums of money, increasingly larger, with the threat that she would make a disclosure if he didn't pay. He paid. Then, Sunday evening, night before last, she asked for fifty thousand dollars. Harassed beyond endurance, he came to me for help. He gave me, I think—me and Mr. Goodwin—a correct and accurate account as far as it went, but not a complete one. He did not tell me that Miss Murphy had somehow found out who and what and where his daughter was, though he must have known that she had. In any event, I know it, having deduced it."

58

Wolfe stopped for an extra breath and went on, "There was another thing that Mr. Perrit almost certainly knew, since everything connected with his daughter was of special concern to him, but didn't tell me. Miss Murphy, out West, had been attached to a young man, or he had been attached to her, or both. He came to New York—I don't know when, but it may be surmised that it was about the time Miss Murphy began demanding money from Mr. Perrit—probably shortly before that—and he and Miss Murphy resumed their—friendship. From Miss Murphy the young man learned the identity of Mr. Perrit's daughter and decided on a stroke of his own. Unknown to Miss Murphy, he contrived to meet the daughter, to pursue a friendship with her, to ask her to marry him, and to be accepted. He had enough education and temerity to masquerade as a law student, and indeed, his temerity was unlimited. He didn't bother about an alias. I suppose at the beginning, he regarded the two worlds as too far apart ever to get connected, and if he regretted it later on it was too late to change. Anyhow, he became engaged to marry Mr. Perrit's daughter under his own, Morton Schane."

"That's a lie." It was Morton again. His tone wasn't as loud as it had been before, but it packed more weight.

"You'll have a turn, Mr. Schane," Wolfe said. His glance went around. "As I said, I can't believe that Mr. Perrit didn't know about Mr. Schane, though he didn't mention him to me. I presume Mr. Schane calculated that the highest expectations, in the long run, would be realized through the real daughter and not the counterfeit one. I assume that although Mr. Perrit knew what Mr. Schane was doing, Miss Murphy didn't, or something would have popped. I also assume that Mr. Perrit had got onto Mr. Schane quite recently, since Mr. Schane had continued his program without interference. I also assume that the reason Mr. Perrit didn't mention Mr. Schane to me was because he was confident of being able to handle that himself, by his own methods."

"You assume," Morton sneered.

Wolfe nodded. "I agree. These presumptions and assumptions are merely embroidery and really not needed." He kept his eyes on Morton. "Their only purpose is to answer the question, why? Why did you shoot and kill Miss Murphy and Mr. Perrit? Merely to clear the track, to get them out of the way, since the daughter was betrothed to you? Possibly, but I doubt it. More probably, something had happened; you had become aware of some deadly threat. One more assumption—"

Morton stood up. "You'll eat all this, you fat, lying, son-of-a-bitch! I'm going!"

Fabian stood up.

Meeker stood up.

Morton Schane didn't move.

Fabian asked, "You got anything else?"

"Nothing but proof," Wolfe told him, but his eyes stuck to Schane. "Last evening Mr. Perrit's daughter and this young man dined with us. One or two remarks he made stirred a faint suspicion in me. It was very faint, the merest breath, but it was simple to test him. He was in his last year at law school. I asked him if he had learned to draft torts, and he said he had. A tort is an act, not a document, as any law student would know. You can't draft a tort any more than you can draft a burglary. That settled him. I had my chef save his wineglass, and after Mr. Schane had left I got in touch with Mr. Panzer and made various arrangements. One resulted in our learning, through the FBI and their fingerprint files, of Mr. Schane's background and record. Another arrangement, that Mr. Panzer should pick up Mr. Schane last evening in front of the building where Mr. Perrit's daughter lives, and keep on his trail—"

Morton still had his temerity. His hand went for his hip like a frog for a fly. He did get his gun out, because Fabian's first bullet missed, and he even pulled the trigger, but all he hit was plaster. Then he splashed back on the couch, pulling the trigger again. By that time Meeker was shooting too, which I have never understood, but it was something never seen before and surely never will be again—Fabian and Thumbs

Meeker blazing away at the same target. Morton slithered off of the couch onto the floor. That was his last move.

XIII

Six days later, Monday again, Wolfe came down from the plant rooms at six o'clock, negotiated himself into his chair behind his desk, and rang for beer.

I turned away from my typewriter and spoke. "The evening paper says that the District Attorney has decided not to charge Meeker or Fabian because a man has a right to defend himself, and all witnesses agree that Schane shot first."

"Perfectly sound," Wolfe murmured.

"Sure. But that reminds me. So far, you have refused to loosen up. I would like to make it clear that I do not believe that Saul was on Schane's tail that night. He damn well didn't tail him through Seventy-eighth Street, nor later through our street, either, when Schane was in his hot taxicab. I think you put that in because you knew it was the one thing that was sure to make Schane go for his gun."

"Not sound at all. Mere conjecture."

"I like it. Another thing. I now think you did have a program. I think you invited Schwartz to come at two o'clock because you wanted a witness, not me who works for you, to what you said to Fabian. You intended to tell Fabian a good deal, maybe everything, about Schane, but do it in such a way that you couldn't be charged with incitement to crime. You could be doing it just to put us in the clear. You didn't have a thing on Schane for the murders. You didn't know then that he was fool enough to go on carrying the gun he had killed them with. You knew Fabian would get Schane, and so your ward wouldn't marry him, which you didn't approve of. You thought Beulah was so hipped on him that she would take him in spite of his past—since the killings couldn't be pinned on him—whereas the fact was that after she had seen me he was just a vague spot to her."

"Shut up. I want to read."

"Yes, sir. In an hour or so. Then Schane came here with her and insisted on joining us in the office, and right away you began to ad lib. You figured that with Fabian and Saul and me all here, one of us was bound to plug him before he plugged you. By the way, in the excitement I didn't see Saul shoot at all, but it was his bullet that went through the middle of Schane's pump and lodged in his spine. When Meeker showed up too I suppose you thought there was nothing to it, which speaks louder for your optimism than it does for your mathematics. If I had known how you had it sketched I would have offered twelve for five that he would get you, at least some part of you, before he was stopped. I had seen him in action, shooting out of car windows in dim street light."

Wolfe sighed. "I suppose you have to get it out of your system."

"I do, and this is the day for it. With meat controls taken off last night, what is there to fear? But I am willing to be rode too, because on one count I have it coming. I told you that just before Violet quit for good, while I was kneeling there by her, she said, "It's a shame. Shame!' Of course she didn't. What she said was, 'It's Schane. Schane!' I fumbled that one, and hereafter I'll wash my ears better. Now I suppose you'll tell me that you knew—"

The phone rang. I got it, used the customary formula, and a voice came.

"May I speak to Mr. Harold Stevens?"

"He's not in," I said courteously. "Gone to Central Park for his health. Will anyone else do?"

"You might if you weren't so busy. When I was down there Friday signing those papers you were too busy to offer to drive me home. Harold Stevens always drove me home."

"Naturally. Harold was on the make. He was after money. I shy off from rich women because I am not a dough-hound. Was there any particular problem?"

"No, nothing, except that I started to decide where to go for dinner, and I'm sick of all the restaurants around here, and—"

"Not another word. I know just how you feel. You were wishing you didn't have to eat alone, and I was

wishing I didn't have to eat with the person I was going to eat with. Meet me at seven o'clock at Ribeiro's, Fifty-second Street east of Lexington, downtown side. Got it?"

"Yes, but I didn't—"

"Certainly you did. So did I. I'll be at the bar. I don't suppose you can properly go dancing for two or three years, but we're resourceful. We can sit somewhere and talk about health—oh, no, that's Harold. Seven o'clock?"

"Sure."

I hung up and told Wolfe, "Okay, go on and read. I'm going up and change my shirt. I'm dining with your new ward, but don't jump to the conclusion that I'm thinking of marrying her. I don't want you dragging Fabian and Thumbs Meeker down here again on my account."

2 | Help Wanted, Male

I

HE PAID us a visit the day he stopped the bullet.

Ben Jensen was a publisher, a politician, and in my opinion a poop. I had had a sneaking idea that he would have gone ahead and bought the inside Army dope that Captain Peter Root had offered to sell him if he had been able to figure out a way of using it without any risk of losing a hunk of hide. But he had played it safe and had co-operated with Nero Wolfe like a good little boy. That had been a couple of months before.

Now, early on a Tuesday morning, he phoned to say he wanted to see Wolfe. When I told him that Wolfe would be occupied with the orchids, as usual, until eleven o'clock, he fussed a little and made a date for eleven sharp. He arrived five minutes ahead of time, and I escorted him into the office and invited him to deposit his big bony frame in the red leather chair.

After he sat down he asked me, "Don't I remember you? Aren't you Major Goodwin?"

"Yep."

"You're not in uniform."

"I was just noticing," I said, "that you need a haircut. At your age, with your gray hair, it looks better trimmed. More distinguished. Shall we continue with the personal remarks?"

There was the clang of Wolfe's personal elevator out in the hall, and a moment later Wolfe entered, exchanged greetings with the caller, and got himself, all of his two hundred and sixty-some pounds, lowered into his personal chair behind his desk.

Ben Jensen said, "Something I wanted to show

you—got it in the mail this morning," and took an envelope from his pocket and stood up to hand it across. Wolfe glanced at the envelope, removed a piece of paper from it and glanced at that, and passed them along to me. The envelope was addressed to Ben Jensen, neatly hand-printed in ink. The piece of paper had been clipped from something, all four edges, with scissors or a sharp knife, and it had printed on it, not by hand, in large black script:

YOU ARE ABOUT TO DIE
AND I WILL WATCH YOU DIE!

Wolfe murmured, "Well, sir?"

"I can tell you," I put in, "free for nothing, where this came from."

Jensen snapped at me. "You mean who sent it?"

"Oh, no. For that I would charge. It was clipped from an ad for a movie called *Meeting at Dawn*. The movie of the century. I saw the ad last week in the *American Magazine*. I suppose it's in all the magazines. If you could find—"

Wolfe made a noise at me and murmured again at Jensen, "Well, sir?"

"What am I going to do?" Jensen demanded.

"I'm sure I don't know. Have you any notion who sent it?"

"No. None at all." Jensen sounded grieved. "Damn it, I don't like it. It's not just the usual junk from an anonymous crank. Look at it! It's direct and to the point. I think someone's going to try to kill me, and I don't know who or why or when or how. I suppose tracing it is out of the question, but I want some protection. I want to buy it from you."

I put up a hand to cover a yawn. I knew there would be nothing doing—no case, no fee, no excitement. In the years I had been living in Nero Wolfe's house on West Thirty-fifth Street, acting as a goad, prod, lever, irritant, and chief assistant in the detective business, I had heard him tell at least fifty scared people, of all conditions and ages, that if someone had determined to kill them and was going to be stubborn about it he would probably succeed. On occasion, when the bank balance was doing a dive, he had furnished Cather or Durkin or Panzer or Keems as a bodyguard at a hundred per cent mark-up, but now they were all fighting Germans or Japs, and anyhow, we had just deposited a five-figure check from a certain client.

Jensen got sore, naturally, but Wolfe only murmured at him that he might succeed in interesting the police or that we would be glad to give him a list of reliable detective agencies which would provide companions for his movements as long as he remained alive—at sixty bucks for twenty-four hours. Jensen said that wasn't it, he wanted to hire Wolfe's brains. Wolfe merely made a face and shook his head. Then Jensen wanted to know what about Goodwin? Wolfe said that Major Goodwin was an officer in the United States Army.

"He's not in uniform," Jensen growled.

Wolfe was patient. "Officers in Military Intelligence on special assignments," he explained, "have freedoms. Major Goodwin's special assignment is to assist me in various projects entrusted to me by the Army. For which I am not paid. I have little time now for my private business. I think, Mr. Jensen, you should move and act with reasonable precaution for a while. For example, in licking the flaps of envelopes—such things as that. Examine the strip of mucilage. Nothing is easier than to remove the mucilage from an envelope flap and replace it with a mixture containing a deadly poison. Any door you open, anywhere, stand to one side and fling the door wide with a push or a pull before crossing the sill. Things like that."

"Good God!" Jensen muttered.

Wolfe nodded. "That's how it is. But keep in mind that this fellow has severely restricted himself, if he's not a liar. He says he will watch you die. That greatly limits him in method and technique. He or she has to be there when it happens. So I advise prudence and a decent vigilance. Use your brains, but give up the idea of renting mine. No panic is called for. Archie, how many people have threatened to take my life in the past ten years?"

I pursed my lips. "Oh, maybe twenty-two."

"Pfui." He scowled at me. "At least a hundred. And I am not dead yet, Mr. Jensen."

Jensen pocketed his clipping and envelope and departed, no better off than when he came except for the valuable advice about licking envelopes and opening doors. I felt kind of sorry for him and took the trouble to wish him good luck as I escorted him to the front and let him out to the street, and even used some breath to tell him that if he decided to try an agency Cornwall and Mayer had the best men. Then I went back to the office and stood in front of Wolfe's desk, facing him, and pulled my shoulders back and expanded my chest. I took that attitude because I had some news to break to him and thought it might help to look as much like an Army officer as possible.

"I have an appointment," I said, "at nine o'clock Thursday morning, in Washington, with General Carpenter."

Wolfe's brows went up a millimeter. "Indeed?"

"Yes, sir. At my request. I wish to take an ocean trip. I want to get a look at a German. I would like to catch one, if it can be done without much risk, and pinch him and make some remarks to him. I have thought up a crushing remark to make to a German and would like to use it."

"Nonsense." Wolfe was placid. "Your three requests to be sent overseas have been denied."

"Yeah, I know." I kept my chest out. "But that was just colonels and old Fife. Carpenter will see my point, I admit you're a great detective, the best orchid-grower in New York, a champion eater and beer-drinker, and a genius. But I've been working for you a hundred years—anyhow, a lot of years—and this is a hell of a way to spend a war. I'm going to see General Carpenter and lay it out. Of course he'll phone you. I appeal to your love of country, your vanity, your finer instincts—what there is of them—and your dislike of Germans. If you tell Carpenter it would be impossible for you to get along without me, I'll put pieces of gristle in your crabmeat and sugar in your beer."

Wolf opened his eyes and glared at me. The mere suggestion of sugar in his beer made him speechless.

I sat down and said in a pleasant conversational tone, "I told Jensen that Cornwall and Mayer is the best agency."

Wolfe grunted. "He'll waste his money. I doubt the urgency of his peril. A man planning a murder doesn't spend his energy clipping pieces out of advertisements of motion pictures."

That was Tuesday. The next morning, Wednesday, the papers headlined the murder of Ben Jensen on the front page. Eating breakfast in the kitchen with Fritz, as usual, I was only halfway through the report in the *Times* when the doorbell rang, and when I answered it I found on the stoop our old friend Inspector Cramer of the Homicide Squad.

II

Nero Wolfe said, "Not interested, not involved, and not curious."

He was a sight, as he always was when propped up in bed with his breakfast tray. The custom was for Fritz to deliver the tray to his room on the second floor at eight o'clock. It was now eight-fifteen, and already down the gullet were the peaches and cream, most of the unrationed bacon, and two-thirds of the eggs, not to mention coffee and the green tomato jam. The black silk coverlet was folded back, and you had to look to tell where the yellow percale sheet ended and the yellow pajamas began. Few people except Fritz and me ever got to see him like that, but he had stretched a point for Inspector Cramer, who knew that from nine to eleven he would be up in the plant rooms with the orchids and unavailable.

"In the past dozen years," Cramer said in his ordinary growl, without any particular feeling, "you have told me, I suppose, in round figures, ten million lies."

The commas were chews on his unlighted cigar. He looked the way he always did when he had been working all night—peevish and put upon but under control, all except his hair, which had forgotten where the part went.

Wolfe, who was hard to rile at breakfast, swallowed toast and jam and then coffee, ignoring the insult.

Cramer said, "He came to see you yesterday morning, twelve hours before he was killed. You don't deny that."

"And I have told you what for," Wolfe said politely. "He had received that threat and said he wanted to hire my brains. I declined to work for him and he went away. That was all."

"Why did you decline to work for him? What had he done to you?"

"Nothing." Wolfe poured coffee. "I don't do that kind of work. A man whose life is threatened anonymously is either in no danger at all, or his danger is so acute and so ubiquitous that his position is hopeless. My only previous association with Mr. Jensen was in connection with an attempt by an Army captain named Peter Root to sell him inside Army information for political purposes. Together we got the necessary evidence and Captain Root was court-martialed. Mr. Jensen was impressed, so he said, by my handling of that case. I suppose that was why he came to me when he wanted help."

"Did he think the threat came from someone connected with Captain Root?"

"No. Root wasn't mentioned. He said he had no idea who intended to kill him."

Cramer humphed. "That's what he told Tim Cornwall too. Cornwall thinks you passed because you knew or suspect it was too hot to handle. Naturally Cornwall is bitter. He has lost his best man."

"Indeed," Wolfe said mildly. "If that was his best man . . ."

"So Cornwall says," Cramer insisted, "and he's dead. Name of Doyle, been in the game twenty years, with a good record. The picture as we've got it doesn't necessarily condemn him. Jensen went to Cornwall and Mayer yesterday about noon, and Cornwall assigned Doyle as a guard. We've traced all their movements— nothing special. In the evening, Doyle went along to a meeting at a midtown club. They left the club at eleven-twenty, and apparently went straight home, on the subway or a bus, to the apartment house where Jensen lived on Seventy-third Street near Madison. It was eleven-forty-five when they were found dead on the sidewalk at the entrance to the apartment house.

Both shot in the heart with a thirty-eight, Doyle from behind and Jensen from the front. We have the bullets. No powder marks. No nothing."

Wolfe murmured sarcastically, putting down his coffee cup and indicating that since I was there I might as well remove the tray, "Mr. Cornwall's best man."

"Nuts," Cramer objected to the sarcasm. "He was shot in the back. There's a narrow passage ten paces away where the guy could have hid. Or the shots could have come from a passing car, or from across the street—though that would have taken some shooting, two right in the pump. We haven't found anybody who heard the shots. The doorman was in the basement stoking the water heater, the excuse for that being that they're short of men like everybody else. The elevator man was on his way to the tenth floor with a passenger, a tenant. The bodies were discovered by two women on their way home from a movie. It must have happened not more than a minute before they came by, but they had just got off a Madison Avenue bus at the corner."

Wolfe got out of bed, which was an operation deserving an audience. He glanced at the clock on the bed table. It was eight-thirty-five.

"I know, I know," Cramer growled. "You've got to get dressed and get upstairs to your goddam horticulture. The tenant going up in the elevator was a prominent doctor who barely knew Jensen by sight. The two women who found the bodies are Seventh Avenue models who never heard of Jensen. The elevator man has worked there over twenty years without displaying a grudge, and Jensen was a generous tipper and popular with the bunch. The doorman is a fat nitwit who was hired two weeks ago only because of the manpower situation and doesn't know the tenants by name. Beyond those, all we have is the population of New York City and the guests who arrive and depart daily and nightly. That's why I came to you, and for God's sake, give me what you've got. You can see I need it."

"Mr. Cramer." The mountain of yellow pajamas moved. "I repeat. I am not interested, not involved, and not curious." Wolfe headed for the bathroom.

Two minutes later, downstairs, as I opened the front door for Inspector Cramer's exit, he turned to me with

70

his cigar tilted up from the corner of his mouth to about a quarter to one and observed, "One thing about that black silk bed cover, it can be used for his shroud when the time comes. Let me know, and I'll come and help sew on it."

I eyed him coldly. "You scold us when we lie, and you scold us when we tell the truth. What does the city pay you for anyhow?"

Back in the office there was the morning mail, which had been ignored on account of the interruption of the early visitor. I got busy with the opener. There was the usual collection of circulars, catalogues, appeals, requests for advice without enclosed check, and other items, fully up to the pre-war standard, and I was getting toward the bottom of the stack without encountering anything startling or promising when I slit another envelope and there it was.

I stared at it. I picked up the envelope and stared at that. I don't often talk to myself, but I said loud enough for me to hear, "My goodness." Then I left the rest of the mail for later and went and mounted the three flights to the plant rooms on the roof. Proceeding through the first three departments, past everything from rows of generating flasks to Cattleya hybrids covered with blooms, I found Wolfe in the potting room, with Theodore Horstmann, the orchid nurse, examining a crate of sphagnum that had just arrived.

"Well?" he demanded with no sign of friendliness. The general idea was that when he was up there I interrupted him at my peril.

"I suppose," I said carelessly, "that I shouldn't have bothered you, but I ran across something in the mail that I thought you'd find amusing," and I put them on the bench before him, side by side: the envelope with his name and address printed on it by hand, in ink, and the piece of paper that had been clipped from something with scissors or a sharp knife, reading in large black script, printed but not by hand:

YOU ARE ABOUT TO DIE—
AND I WILL WATCH YOU DIE!

"It sure is a coincidence," I remarked, grinning at him.

71

III

I thought he would at least mutter "Indeed," but he didn't. He looked at the exhibits for a moment without touching them, sent me a sharp glance indicating an instantaneous suspicion that I was implicated, and said without any perceptible quiver, "I'll look over the mail at eleven o'clock as usual."

It was the grand manner all right. Seeing he was impervious, I retrieved the exhibits without a word, returned to the office, and busied myself with the chores—letters to write, vital statistics of orchids to enter on cards, and similar manly tasks. Nor did he fudge on the time. It was eleven on the dot when he came down, got into his oversized chair behind his desk, and began the routine—going through the mail I had not discarded, signing checks, inspecting the bank balance, dictating letters and memos, glancing at his calendar pad, and ringing for beer. Not until Fritz had brought the beer and he had irrigated his interior did he lean back in his chair, let his eyes go half shut, and observe:

"Archie, you could easily have clipped that thing from the magazine, bought an envelope and printed my name and address on it, stamped it and mailed it. Nothing would have been simpler."

I grinned at him and shook my head. "Not my style. Besides, what for? I never exert myself without a purpose. Besides again, would I be apt to infuriate and embitter you at this moment, when I know General Carpenter will phone for your opinion?"

"You will, of course, postpone your trip to Washington."

I let my frank, open countenance betray surprise. "I can't. I have an appointment with a lieutenant general. Anyhow, why?" I indicated the envelope and clipping on his desk. "That tomfoolery? No panic is called for. I doubt the urgency of your peril. A man planning a murder doesn't spend his energy clipping pieces out of adver—"

"You are going to Washington?"

"Yes, sir. I have a date. Of course I could phone

Carpenter and tell him your nerves are a little shaky on account of an anony—"

"When do you leave?"

"I have a seat on the six o'clock train, but I could take a later—"

"Very well. Then we have the day. Your notebook."

Wolfe leaned forward to pour beer and drink, and then leaned back again. "I offer a comment on your jocosity. When Mr. Jensen called here yesterday and showed us that thing we had no inkling of the character of the person who had sent it. It might have been merely the attempt of a coward to upset his digestion. We no longer enjoy that ignorance. This person not only promply killed Mr. Jensen, with wit equal to his determination, but also killed Mr. Doyle, a stranger, whose presence could not have been foreseen. We now know that this person is cold-blooded, ruthless, quick to decide and to act, and an egomaniac."

"Yes, sir. I agree. If you go to bed and stay there until I get back from Washington, letting no one but Fritz enter the room, I may not be able to control my tongue when with you but actually I will understand and I won't tell anybody. You need a rest anyway. And don't lick any envelopes."

"Bah." Wolfe wiggled a finger at me. "That thing was not sent to you. Presumably you are not on the agenda."

"Yes, sir."

"And this person is dangerous and requires attention."

"I agree."

"Very well." Wolfe shut his eyes. "Take notes as needed. It may be assumed, if this person means business with me as he did with Mr. Jensen, that this is connected with the case of Captain Peter Root. I had no other association whatever with Mr. Jensen—learn the whereabouts of Captain Root."

"The court-martial gave him three years in the cooler."

"I know it. Is he there? Also, what about that young woman his fiancée who raised such a ruction about it and called me a mongrel bloodhound? A contradiction in terms—not a good epithet. Her name is Jane Geer."

Wolfe's eyes half opened for an instant. "You have a habit of knowing how to locate a personable young woman without delay. Have you seen that one recently?"

"Oh," I said offhand, "I sort of struck up an acquaintance with her. I guess I can get in touch with her. But I doubt—"

"Do so. I want to see her. Excuse me for interrupting, but you have a train to catch. Also inform Inspector Cramer of this development and suggest that he investigate Captain Root's background—his relatives and intimates—anyone besides Miss Geer who might thirst for vengeance at his disgrace. I'll do that. If Captain Root is in prison arrange with General Fife to bring him here. I want to have a talk with him. Where is the clipping received yesterday by Mr. Jensen? Ask Mr. Cornwall and Mr. Cramer. There is the possibility that this is not another one like it, but the same one."

I shook my head. "No, sir. This one is clipped closer to the printing at the upper right."

I noticed that, but ask anyway. Inspect the chain bolts on the doors and test the night gong in your room. Fritz will sleep in your room tonight. I shall speak to Fritz and Theodore. All of this can easily be attended to by telephone except Miss Geer, and that is your problem. Do not for the present mention her to Mr. Cramer. I want to see her before he does. When will you return from Washington?"

"I should be able to catch a noon train back—my appointment's at nine. Getting here around five." I added earnestly, "If I can clear it with Carpenter to cross the ocean, I will of course arrange not to leave until this ad-clipper has been attended to. I wouldn't want—"

"Don't hurry back on my account. Or alter your plans. You receive a salary from the government." Wolfe's tone was dry, sharp, and icy, plainly intended to pierce all my vital organs at once. He went on with it, "Please get General Fife on the phone. We'll begin by learning about Captain Root."

The program went smoothly, all except the Jane Geer number. If it hadn't been for her I'd have been able to make the six o'clock train with hours to spare.

Fife reported back on Root in thirty minutes, to the effect that Root was in the clink on government property down in Maryland and would be transported to New York without delay for an interview with Wolfe, which appeared to contradict the saying that democracies are always ungrateful. Cornwall said he had turned the clipping and envelope Jensen had received over to Inspector Cramer, and Cramer verified it and said he had it. But Cramer seemed to be too busy for an extended phone conversation, and I understood why when, shortly after we had finished lunch, he arrived at our place in person, sat down in the red leather chair and narrowed his eyes at Wolfe, emitted a hoarse, grating chuckle and said offensively:

"Interested, involved, and curious."

Naturally Wolfe tossed it back at him but after three minutes of fast and hot tongue work they patched it up and discussed matters. Cramer had the Jensen clipping with him, and they compared the two and found they were from copies of the same magazine, a piece of information which I would have considered no bargain at a nickel. We emptied the bag on the Captain Root episode, all but the Jane Geer item, and Cramer said he would do a survey of Root's history and connections. As for the official investigation of the Jensen murder, they still had the entire population of the metropolitan area for suspects, which gave them plenty of room to move around in. When Cramer's recital made it evident that the squad had got nowhere at all, Wolfe saw fit to make a couple of cracks and Cramer returned the compliment, so the conference ended on the same breezy note it had begun with.

On Jane Geer the luck was low. When before noon I phoned the advertising agency she worked for I was told that she was somewhere on Long Island admiring some client's product for which she was to produce copy. When I finally did get her, after four o'clock, she went willful on me, presumably because she regarded my phoning five times in one day as evidence that my primal impulses had been aroused and I was beginning to pant. She would not come to Nero Wolfe's place unless I went after her and bought her a cocktail first. So

75

I met her a little after five at the Calico Room at the Churchill, and bought.

She had put in a full day's work, but looking at her you might have thought she had come straight from an afternoon nap and a relaxing bath.

It was not my opinion, at that stage of affairs, that this special item of God's second-thought bounty for man was guilty of premeditated and cold-blooded murder. Because of my interest in human nature I had found occasion, in the brief period since I had first met her, to discover that she was capable of strong feelings over a wide range of territory, and that she did not believe in limiting their expression to little hints like darting the eyes. I had never seen her scratch or pull hair, but I had known her only two months or so, and unquestionably she packed the potential. However, I felt that the Jensen-Doyle massacre, one of them a perfect stranger, did not belong in her repertory; and I knew she had acquired a different slant on the Captain Root incident since the day she called Wolfe a mongrel bloodhound.

She darted her brown eyes at me. I didn't say she never darted, I said she didn't stop there. "Let me," she said, "see your right forefinger."

I poked it at her. She rubbed its tip gently with the tip of her own. "I wondered if it had a callus. After dialing my number five times in less than five hours. Are you trying to win some kind of a bet? Or did you dream about me?" She sipped her Tom Collins, bending her head to get her lips to the straw. A strand of her hair slipped forward over an eye and a cheek, and I reached across and used the same finger to put it back in place.

"I took that liberty," I told her, "because I wish to have an unobstructed view of your lovely phiz. I want to see if you turn pale and your eyes get glassy."

"Overwhelmed by you so near?"

"No, I know that reaction—I correct for it. Anyhow I doubt if I'm magnetic right now because I'm sore at you for making me miss a train."

"I didn't phone you this time. You phoned me."

"Okay." I drank. "You said on the phone that you still don't like Nero Wolfe and you wouldn't go to see him unless you knew what for and maybe not even then. So this is what for. He wants to ask you whether you intend to kill him yourself or hire the same gang that you got to kill Jensen and Doyle. So he'll know what to expect."

"Mercy." She looked my face over. "You'd better put your humor on a diet. It's taking on weight."

I shook my head. "Ordinarily I would enjoy playing catch with you, as you are aware, but I can't miss all the trains. I'm not even trying to be funny, let alone succeeding. I was instructed to tell you this if necessary. Because Wolfe's life has been threatened in the same manner as Jensen's was, the supposition is that Jensen was murdered for revenge, for what he did to Captain Root. Because of the cutting remarks you made when Root was trapped, and your general attitude, there is a tendency to want to know what you have been doing lately. Wolfe wants to ask you. If you wonder why I didn't start with some grade A detecting by finding out where you were last night between eleven and twelve, that wouldn't help any because what if you hired—"

"Stop." She stopped me. "I'm dreaming."

"I'm not."

"It's fantastic."

"Sure. Lots of things are."

"Nero Wolfe seriously thinks I—did that? Or had it done?"

"I didn't say so. He wants to discuss it with you."

Her eyes flashed. Her tone took on an edge. "It is also extremely corny. And the police? Have you kindly arranged that when Wolfe finishes with me I proceed to headquarters? Would you be good enough to phone my boss in the morning and let him know where I am? I can't begin to tell you—"

"Listen, Tiger-eyes." She let me cut her off, which was a pleasant surprise. "Have you noticed me sneaking up on you from behind? If so, draw it for me. I have explained a situation. Your name has not been mentioned to the police, though they have consulted us. You are, let us assume, as innocent as a cheeping chick, which you do not, however, resemble in visible physical aspects."

"Thank you." The edge was even sharper.

"You're welcome. But since the police are onto the Root angle they are apt to get a steer in your direction without us, and it wouldn't hurt if Wolfe had already satisfied himself that you wouldn't kill a fly."

"By what process?" She was scornful. "I suppose he asks me if I ever committed murder, and I smile and say no, and he apologizes and gives me an orchid."

"Not quite. He's a genius. He asks you questions like do you bait your own hook when you go fishing, and you reveal yourself without knowing it."

"It sounds fascinating. " Her eyes suddenly changed, and the line of her lips. She had been struck with an idea. "I wonder," she said.

"What is it, and we'll both wonder."

"Sure." Her eyes had changed more. "This wouldn't by any chance be a climax you've been working up to? You with a thousand girls and women so that you have to issue ration books so many minutes to a coupon, and yet finding so much time for me? Leading up, heaven knows why, and I don't care to go to heaven to find out, to this idiotic frame—"

"Turn that one off," I broke in, "or I'll begin to get suspicious myself. You know darned well why I have found time for you, having a mirror as you do. I have been experimenting to test my emotional reaction to form, color, touch, and various perfumes, and I have been deeply grateful for your co-operation. For you to pretend to imagine that the experiment we have been carrying on was on my part preparation for a frame-up for murder is an insult both to my intelligence and my emotional integrity."

"Ha, ha." She stood up, her eyes not softening nor her tone melting. "I am going to see Nero Wolfe. I welcome an opportunity to reveal myself to Nero Wolfe. Do I go or are you taking me?"

I took her. I paid the check and we went out and got a taxi.

During the brief ride downtown and crosstown she got more realistic. She said, among other things, "I was taken in by Peter Root. I thought he was innocent and was being made the goat. So I expressed myself accordingly, and why shouldn't I? But I am over all that, as you know unless you are a two-faced subhuman Pithecanthropus, and this business about the murder of that Jensen, which I read about in the morning paper, is utter poppycock. I'm a working girl. After my experience with the charming, irresistible Peter I wouldn't marry a combination of Winston Churchill and Victor Mature. I wouldn't even marry you. I have a future. I intend to become the first female vice-president of the biggest advertising agency in the country. I never will, or anyway not for years, if my name is made public as a suspect in a murder case. The publicity about me in the Peter Root business didn't help me any, and this would about finish me."

"Don't," I advised her, "take that line with Nero Wolfe. His attitude toward women as business executives is a little peculiar, not to mention his attitude toward women."

"I'll handle Nero Wolfe."

"Hooray. No one ever has yet."

I didn't get to see her try, because she didn't get to see Wolfe.

Since chain-bolt orders were in effect, my key wouldn't let us in and I had to ring the doorbell for Fritz. I had just pushed the button when who should appear, mounting the steps to join us on the stoop, but the Army officer that they use for a model when they want to do a picture conveying the impression that masculine comeliness will win the war. I admit he was handsome; I admitted it to myself right then, when I first saw him. He looked preoccupied and concentrated, but even so he found time for a glance at Jane, which was actually nothing against him, especially when you consider that she also found time for a glance at him.

At that moment the door swung open and I spoke to Fritz. "Okay, thanks. Is Mr. Wolfe in the office?"

"No, he's up in his room."

"All right, I'll take it." Fritz departed, and I maneuvered into position to dominate the scene, on the doorsill facing out. I spoke to the masculine model.

"Yes, Major? This is Nero Wolfe's place."

"I know it is." He had a baritone voice that suited him to a T. "I want to see him. My name is Emil Jensen. I am the son of Ben Jensen, who was killed last night."

"Oh." There wasn't much resemblance, but that's nature's lookout. I have enough to do. "Mr. Wolfe has an appointment. It would be handy if I could tell him what you want."

"I want to—consult him. If you don't mind, I'd rather tell him." He smiled to take the sting off. Probably Psychological Warfare Branch.

"I'll see. Come on in." I made room for Jane and he followed her. After attending to the bolt I escorted them to the office, invited them to sit, and went to the phone on my desk and buzzed Wolfe's room extension.

"Yes?" Wolfe's voice came.

"Archie. Miss Geer is here. Also Major Emil Jensen just arrived. He is the son of Ben Jensen and prefers to tell you what he wants to consult you about."

"Give them both my regrets. I am engaged and can see no one."

"Engaged for how long?"

"Indefinitely. I can make no appointments for this week."

"But you may remember—"

"Archie! Tell them that, please." The line died.

So I told them that. They were not pleased. The Lord knows what kind of a performance Jane would have put on if she hadn't been restrained by the presence of a stranger; as it was, she didn't have to fumble around for pointed remarks. Jensen wasn't indignant, but he sure was stubborn. During an extended conversation that got nowhere, I noticed a gradual increase in their inclination to cast sympathetic glances at each other, which I suppose was only natural since they were both in a state of irritation at the same person for the same reason. I thought it might help matters along, meaning they might clear out sooner, if I changed the subject, so I said emphatically, "Miss Geer, this is Major Jensen."

He got to his feet, bowed to her like a man who knows how to bow, and told her, "How do you do. It looks as if it's hopeless, at least for this evening, for both of us. I'll have to hunt a taxi, and it would be a pleasure if you'll let me drop you . . ."

So they left together. Going down the stoop, which I admit was moderately steep, he indicated not obstrusively that he had an arm there, and she rested her fingers in the bend of it to steady herself. That alone showed astonishing progress in almost no time at all, for she was by no means a born clinger.

Oh, well, he was a major too. I shrugged indifferently as I shut the door. Then I sought the stairs, mounted a flight to the door of Wolfe's room, knocked, and was invited to enter.

Standing in the doorway to his bathroom, facing me, his old-fashioned razor in his hand, all lathered up, he demanded brusquely, "What time is it?"

"Six-thirty."

"When is the next train?"

"Seven o'clock. But what the hell, apparently there is going to be work to do. I can put it off to next week."

"No. It's on your mind. Get that train."

"I have room in my mind for—"

"No."

I tried one more stab. "My motive is selfish. If while I am sitting talking to Carpenter in the morning word comes that you have been killed or even temporarily disabled he'll blame me and I won't stand a chance. So for purely selfish reasons—"

"Confound it," he barked. "You'll miss that train! I have no intention of getting killed. Get out of here!"

I faded, mounted another flight to my room, got into my uniform, and tossed some things into a bag. Boy, was he carrying the banner high! My hero. I caught the train with two minutes to spare.

IV

After the war I intend to run for Congress and put through laws about generals. I have a theory that generals should be rubbed liberally with neat's-foot oil before being taken out and shot. Though I doubt if I would have bothered with the oil in the case of General Carpenter that morning if I had had a free hand.

I was a major. So I sat and said yessir, yessir, yessir, while he told me that he had given me the appointment only because he thought I wanted to discuss something of importance, and that I would stay where I was put, and that the question of my going overseas had been decided long ago and I would shut my trap about it. I never found out whether Wolfe had phoned him or not. He didn't phone Wolfe. He didn't even pat me on the head and tell me there, there, be a good soldier. He merely said, in effect, nuts. Then he observed that since I was in Washington I might as well confer with the staff on various cases, finished and unfinished, and would I report immediately to Colonel Dickey.

I doubt if I made a good impression, considering my state of mind. They kept me around, conferring, all day Thursday and most of Friday. I phoned Wolfe that I was detained. By explaining the situation on Thirty-fifth Street I could have got permission to beat it back to New York, but I wasn't going to give that collection of brass headgear an excuse to giggle around that Nero Wolfe didn't have brains enough to arrange to keep on breathing, in his own house, without me there to look after him. Besides, I knew that Carpenter would have phoned Wolfe, out of courtesy as well as concern, and Wolfe's reaction to that when I got back would be apt to displease me.

But I was tempted to hop a plane when, late Thursday evening, I saw the ad in the *Star*. I had been too busy all day, and at dinner with a bunch of them and after, to take a look at a New York paper. I was alone in my hotel room when it caught my eye, bordered and spaced to make a spot:

WANTED A MAN

weighing about 260-270, around 5 ft. 11, 45-55 years old, medium in coloring, waist not over 48, capable of easy and normal movement. Temporary. Hazardous. $100 a day. Send photo with letter. Box 292 Star.

I read it through four times, stared at it disapprovingly for an additional two minutes, and then reached for the phone and put in a New York call. It was going on midnight, but Wolfe never went to bed early. But when the connection was made, after a short wait, it wasn't his voice that I heard. It was Fritz Brenner's.

"Mr. Nero Wolfe's residence."

Fritz, who had been with Wolfe even longer than me, had his own ideas about certain details. When he answered the phone in the daytime between nine and five he said, "Mr. Nero Wolfe's office." At any other time he said, "Mr. Nero Wolfe's residence."

"Hello, Fritz. Archie. Calling from Washington. Where's Mr. Wolfe?"

"He's in bed. He had a hard day. And evening."

"Doing what?"

He was very busy on the telephone. Also some callers. Mr. Cramer. And he had that stenographer from that place."

"Oh. He did. Using my typewriter. Do you happen to know whether he looked at the *Star* today?"

"The *Star*?" Fritz hesitated. "Not that I know of. He never does. There is only my copy, and it's in the kitchen."

"Get it, and look at an ad, a small one in a box, near the lower right corner on page eleven. Read it. I'll hold the wire."

I sat and waited. Before long he was back on.

"I read it." He sounded puzzled. "Are you calling clear from Washington to make a joke?"

"I am not. I don't feel like joking. The Army won't let me go anywhere. They turned me down. As you read the ad, who did it make you think of?"

"Well—it entered my mind that it was just about a good description of Mr. Wolfe."

"Yeah, it entered mine too. If whoever wrote that wasn't thinking of Nero Wolfe, I'll eat it. First thing in the morning, show it to him. Tell him it looks to me— no, just show it to him. It would annoy him to be told how it looks to me. Anyhow, it will look to him the same way. How's everything?"

"All right."

"The bolts and the gong and so forth?"

"Yes. With you away—"

"I'll be back tomorrow—I hope. Probably late afternoon."

Getting ready for bed, I tried to figure out in what manner, if I were making preparations to kill Nero Wolfe, I could make use of an assistant, hired on a temporary basis at a hundred bucks a day, who was a physical counterpart of Wolfe. The two schemes I devised weren't very satisfactory, and the one I hit on after I got my head on the pillow was even worse, so I flipped the switch on the nervous system and let the muscles quit.

In the morning I went to the Pentagon Building and started conferring again, but it was a lot of hooey. There wasn't anything they really needed me for, and I didn't pretend, even to be polite, that I needed them. Still it went on. By three in the afternoon they seemed to be taking me for granted, as if I belonged there. A feeling that I was doomed began to ooze into me. The Pentagon had got me and would never turn me loose. I was on my way down its throat, and once it got me into its stomach and the machinery began to churn me and squirt dissolving juice over me . . .

At five o'clock I called up all my reserves and told a colonel, "Looky. Don't you think, sir, I've done all I can here? Would it not be advisable for me to return to my post in New York?"

"Well." He lifted his chin to consider. "I'll ask Major Zabreskie. He will of course have to consult Colonel Shawn. It will have to go through—when did you get here?"

"Yesterday morning."

"Whom did you see first on arrival?"

"General Carpenter."

"Oh. The devil." He looked worried. "Then it will have to go to him, and he's tied up. I'll tell you what we'd better do."

He told me what we'd better do. I listened attentively, but it didn't register. Doomed was no word for it. I was sunk for the duration, possibly for life. I told him there was no great rush, it could wait till morning. I would ask Major Zabreskie myself, and managed to break away from him. I got into a corridor, made it to

84

the ground floor, used all my faculties, and succeeded in breaking through to the open air. My trained mind and years of experience as a detective got me onto the right bus. Five minutes at the hotel were enough to get my bag and pay my bill, and I shared a taxi to the airport and bought a ticket to New York. Eating could wait.

But it didn't. I did. There was no room on either the six-thirty or the seven-thirty, so, with both appetite and time, I tried four kinds of sandwiches and found them all edible. Finally I got a seat on the eight-thirty plane, and when it landed at La Guardia Field an hour and a half later I began to feel safe. Surely I could elude them in the throngs of the great metropolis. Actually I was offering ten to one that by morning everybody at the Pentagon would have forgotten that I had been there.

Arriving at Wolfe's house on Thirty-fifth Street a little before eleven, I didn't get out my key because I knew the door would be bolted and I would need help. I gave the button three short pushes as usual, and in a moment there were footsteps, and the curtain was pulled aside, and Fritz was peering at me through the glass panel. Satisfied, he let me in and greeted me with a tone and expression indicating that he was pleased to see me. I saw Wolfe was in the office, since the door to it was open and the light shining through, so I breezed down the hall and on in.

"I am a fug—" I began, and stopped. Wolfe's chair behind his desk, his own chair and no one else's under any circumstances, was occupied by the appropriate mass of matter in comparatively human shape, in other words by a big fat man, but it wasn't Nero Wolfe. I had never seen him before.

V

Fritz, who had stayed to bolt the door, came at me from behind, talking. The occupant of the chair neither moved nor spoke, but merely leered at me. I would have called it a leer. I became aware that Fritz was telling me that Mr. Wolfe was up in his room.

The specimen in the chair said in a husky croak, "I suppose you're Goodwin. Archie. Have a good trip?"

I stared at him. In a way I wished I was back at the Pentagon, and in another way I wished I had come sooner.

He said, "Fritz, bring me another highball."

Fritz said, "Yes, sir."

He said, "Have a good trip, Archie?"

That was enough of that. I marched out to the hall and up a flight, went to Wolfe's door and tapped on it, and called, "Archie!" Wolfe's voice told me to come in, and I entered.

He was seated in his number two chair, under the light, reading a book. He was fully dressed, and there was nothing in his appearance to indicate that he had lost his mind.

I did not intend to give him the satisfaction of sitting there smirking and enjoying fireworks. "Well," I said casually, "I got back. If you're sleepy we can wait till morning for conversation."

"I'm not sleepy." He closed the book with a finger inserted at his page. "Are you going to Europe?"

"You know damn well I'm not." I sat down. "We can discuss that at some future date when I'm out of the Army. It's a relief to find you all alive and well around here. It's very interesting down in Washington. Everybody on their toes."

"No doubt. Did you stop in the office downstairs?"

"I did. So you put that ad in the *Star* yourself. How do you pay him, cash every day? Did you figure out the deductions for income ax and social security? I sat down at my desk and began to report to him. I thought it was you. Until he ordered Fritz to bring him a highball, and I know you hate highballs. Deduction. It reminds me of the time your daughter from Yugoslavia showed up and got us in a mess. Now your twin. At a century per diem it will amount to thirty-six thousand, five hundred—"

"Archie. Shut up."

"Yes, Sir. Shall I go down and chat with him?"

Wolfe put the book down and shifted in his chair with the routine grunts. When the new equilibrium was established he said, "You will find details about him on

86

a slip of paper in the drawer of your desk. He is a re-tired architect named H. H. Hackett, out of funds, and an unsurpassed nincompoop with the manners of a wart hog. I chose him, from those answering the adver-tisement, because his appearance and build were the most suitable and he is sufficiently an ass to be willing to risk his life for a hundred dollars a day."

"If he keeps on calling me Archie the risk will be-come—"

"If you please." Wolfe wiggled a finger at me. "Do you think the idea of him sitting there in my chair is agreeable to me? He may be dead tomorrow or the next day. I told him that. This afternoon he went to Mr. Ditson's place in a taxicab to look at orchids, and came back ostentatiously carrying two plants. Tomor-row afternoon you will drive him somewhere and bring him back, and again in the evening. Dressed for the street, wearing my hat and lightweight coat, carrying my stick, he would deceive anyone except you."

I offered a contribution, deadpan. "I know a young lady, an actress, who would do a swell job of make-up on him if—"

"Archie." His tone was sharp. "Do you think I enjoy this idiotic horseplay?"

"No, sir. But why couldn't you just stay in the house? You do anyway. I've known you not stick your nose out for a month. And be careful who gets in. Until . . ."

"Until what?"

"Until the bird that killed Jensen is caught."

"Bah." He glared at me. "By whom? By Mr. Cramer? What do you suppose he is doing now? Pfui. Major Jensen, Mr. Jensen's son, arriving home on leave from Europe five days ago, learned that during his ab-sence his father had sued his mother for divorce. The father and son quarreled, which was not unique. But Mr. Cramer has a hundred men trying to collect evi-dence that will convict Major Jensen of killing his fa-ther! Utterly intolerable asininity. For what motive could Major Jensen have for killing me, or threatening to?"

"Well, now." My eyebrows were up. "I wouldn't just toss it in the wastebasket. What if the major figured that sending you the same kind of message he sent his father would make everybody react the way you are?"

Wolfe shook his head. "He didn't. Unless he's a born fool. He would have known that merely sending me that thing would be inadequate, that he would have to follow it up by making good on the threat; and he hasn't killed me and I doubt if he intends to. General Fife has looked up his record for me. Mr. Cramer is wasting his time, his men's energy, and the money of the people of New York. I am handicapped. The men I have used and can trust have gone to war. You bounce around thinking only of yourself, deserting me. I am confined to this room, left to my own devices, with a vindictive bloodthirsty maniac waiting for an opportunity to murder me. I have no hint of his identity and no sniff of his scent."

He sure was piling it on. But I knew better than to contribute a note of skepticism when he was in one of his romantic moods, having been fired for that once, and besides, I wouldn't have signed an affidavit that he was exaggerating the situation. So I only asked him, "What about Captain Peter Root? Did they bring him?"

"Yes. He was here today and I talked with him. He has been in that prison for over a month and asserts that this cannot possibly be connected with him or his. He says Miss Geer has not communicated with him for six weeks or more. His mother is teaching school at Danforth, Ohio; that has been verified by Mr. Cramer; she is there. His father, who formerly ran a filling station at Danforth, abandoned wife and son ten years ago, and is said to be working in a war plant in Oklahoma. Wife and son prefer not to discuss him. No brother or sister. According to Captain Root, no one on earth who would conceivably undertake a ride on the subway, let alone multiple murder, to avenge him."

"He might just possibly be right."

"Nonsense. There was no other slightest connection between Mr. Jensen and me. I've asked General Fife to keep Captain Root in New York and to request the prison authorities to look over his effects there if he has any."

"When you get an idea in your head—"

"I never do. As you mean it. I react to stimuli. In this instance I am reacting in the only way open to me. The person who shot Mr. Jensen and Mr. Doyle is bold to the point of rashness. He can probably be tempted to proceed with his program. I am aware that if you drive Mr. Hackett around, and accompany him into the car and out of it, crossing sidewalks at all hours of the day and night, you may get killed. That sort of thing was understood when I employed you and paid you. Now the government pays you. Perhaps Mr. Cramer has a man who resembles you and could be assigned to this. He would have to be a good man, alert and resourceful, for there's no point to this if an attempt on Mr. Hackett's life leaves us as empty-handed as we are now. You can give me your decision in the morning."

I'm surprised that I was able to speak at all. He had of course insulted me a million times, as I had him, but this was worse than an insult, there was no word for it. Coming on top of the turndown I had got in Washington, which had reduced my buoyancy to a record low, it made me so mad that I knew I'd better get out of there. But I did not intend to let him go to bed feeling noble, so I grinned at him and controlled my voice.

"Okay," I told him. "I'll think it over. Sure, Cramer has a lot of good men. Let you know in the morning. I'll remember to turn the gong on."

I went up to my room.

The gong was a dingus under my bed. The custom was that when I retired at night I turned a switch, and if anyone put his foot down in the hall within ten feet of Wolfe's door the gong gonged. It had been installed on account of a certain occurrence some years previously, when Wolfe had got a knife stuck in him. The thing had never gone off except when we tested it, and in my opinion never would, but I never failed to switch it on because if Wolfe had stepped into the hall some night and the gong hadn't sounded it would have caused discussion.

This night, with a stranger in the house, I was glad it was there. I learned from Fritz that H. H. Hackett was sleeping in the south room, on the same floor as me, and on the basis of my brief acquaintance and my one look at him it wouldn't have surprised me if he had undertaken to sneak into Wolfe's room during the night and kill him, dispose of the body down in the furnace, and expect Fritz and me to take him for Wolfe and never catch on. Women and girls of appropriate age and configuration may call me Archie and welcome. With the rest of my fellow beings I am particular. The Hackett person would have had to know me seven years to get the privilege, and I neither desired nor intended that he should know me seven weeks.

In the morning, breakfast was all over the place, with Wolfe in his room, Hackett in the dining-room, and me in the kitchen with Fritz. Afterwards I spent an hour up in the plant rooms with Wolfe, on the matters we usually attended to in the office, together with consideration of the current problem. Wolfe asked if I had decided whether we should get a chauffeur for Hackett from the Homicide Squad.

I looked judicious. "I have," I told him, "thought it over from all angles. Unquestionably Cramer could give us a man who would be my superior in courage, wit, integrity, reflex time, and purity of morals. But here's the trouble—not one anything like as handsome as me. Not a chance. So I'll do it myself."

Wolfe cocked an eye at me. "I meant no offense. My intentions—"

"Forget it. You're under a strain. Mr. Hackett's life is in jeopardy and it makes you nervous."

We got to details. Jane Geer was making a nuisance of herself. I understood now, of course, why Wolfe had refused to see her Wednesday evening. After sending me to get her he had conceived the strategy of hiring a double, and he didn't want her to get a look at the real Nero Wolfe because if she did she would be less likely to be deceived by the counterfeit and go to work on him. That meant she was seriously on his list, but I didn't take the trouble to inform him that in my opinion he could cross her off, since he would only have grunted. She had phoned several times, insisting on seeing him, and had come to the house Friday morning and argued for five minutes with Fritz through the three-inch crack which the chain bolt permitted the door to open to. Now Wolfe had an idea for one of his elaborate charades. I was to phone her to come to see Wolfe at six o'clock that afternoon. When she came I was to take her in to Hackett. Wolfe would coach Hackett for the interview.

I looked skeptical. Wolfe said, "It will give her a chance to kill Mr. Hackett."

I snorted. "With me right there to tell her when to cease firing."

"I admit it is unlikely. Also, it will convince her that Mr. Hackett is me."

"Which still will not shorten his life or lengthen yours."

"Possibly not. Also, it will give me an opportunity to see her and hear her. I shall be at the hole."

So that was really the idea. He would be in the passage, a sort of an alcove, at the kitchen end of the downstairs hall, looking through into the office by means of the square hole in the wall. The hole was camouflaged on the office side by a picture that was transparent one way. He loved to have an excuse to use it, and it actually had been a help now and then.

"That's different," I told him. "If you see her and hear her you'll know she has a heart of platinum."

Major Jensen had phoned once and been told that Wolfe was engaged; apparently he wasn't as persistent as Jane. He had told Cramer that he had come to see Wolfe on Wednesday because on Tuesday morning his father had shown him the threat he had received in the mail and had announced that he was going to consult Nero Wolfe about it; and the major, wishing his father's murderer to be caught and punished, had wanted to talk with Wolfe. It was Wolfe's veto of my suggestion that Major Jensen be invited to call, not on Hackett but on Wolfe himself, that showed me the state he was in. Ordinarily it would have needed no suggestion from me, since the major, in his present situation, was a natural for a fat fee.

When I got down to the office Hackett was there in Wolfe's chair, eating cookies and getting crumbs on the desk. I had told him good morning previously, and having nothing else to tell him, ignored him. From the phone on my desk I got Jane Geer at her office.

"Archie," I told her.

She snapped, "Archie who?"

"Oh, come, come. We haven't sicked the police onto you, have we? Let's gossip a while."

"I am ringing off."

"Then I am too. In a moment. Nero Wolfe wants to see you."

"He does? Ha, ha. He doesn't act like it."

"He has reformed. I showed him a lock of your hair. I showed him a picture of Elsa Maxwell and told him it was you. This time he won't let me come after you."

"Neither will I."

"Okay. Be here at six o'clock and you will be received. Six o'clock today, P.M. Will you?"

She admitted that she would. I made a couple of other calls and did some miscellaneous chores. But I found that my jaw was getting clamped tighter and tighter on account of an irritating noise. Finally I spoke to the occupant of Wolfe's chair. "What kind of cookies are those?"

"Ginger snaps." Evidently the husky croak was his normal voice.

"I didn't know we had any."

"We didn't. I asked Fritz. He doesn't seem to know about ginger snaps, so I walked over to Ninth Avenue and got some."

"When? This morning?"

"Just a little while ago."

I turned to my phone, buzzed the plant rooms, got Wolfe, and told him, "Mr. Hackett is sitting in your chair eating ginger snaps. Just a little while ago he walked to Ninth Avenue and bought them. If he pops in and out of the house whenever he sees fit, what are we getting for our hundred bucks?"

Wolfe spoke to the point. I hung up and turned to Hackett and spoke to the point. He was not to leave the house except as instructed by Wolfe or me. He seemed unimpressed and unconcerned, but nodded good-naturedly.

"All right," he said, "if that's the bargain I'll keep it. But there's two sides to a bargain. I was to be paid daily in advance, and I haven't been paid for today. A hundred dollars net."

Wolfe had told me the same, so I took five twenties from the expense wallet and forked it over.

92

"I must say," he commented, folding the bills neatly and stuffing them in his waistband pocket, "this is a large return for a small effort. I am aware that I may earn it—ah, suddenly and unexpectedly." He leaned toward me. "Though I may tell you confidentially, Archie, that I expect nothing to happen. I am sanguine by nature."

"Yeah," I told him, "me too." I opened the drawer of my desk, the middle one on the right, where I kept armament, got out the shoulder holster and put it on, and selected the gun that was my property—the other two belonged to Wolfe. There were only three cartridges in it, so I pulled the drawer open farther to get to the ammunition compartment and filled the cylinder.

As I shoved the gun into the holster I happened to glance at Hackett and saw that he had a new face. The line of his lips was tight, and his eyes looked startled, wary, and concentrated.

"It hadn't occurred to me before," he said, and his voice had changed too. "This Mr. Wolfe is quite an article, and you're his man. I am doing this with the understanding that someone may mistake me for Mr. Wolfe and try to kill me, but I have only his word for it that that is actually the situation. If it's more complicated than that, and the intention is for you to shoot me yourself, I want to say emphatically that that would not be fair."

I grinned at him sympathetically, trying to make up for my blunder, realizing that I should not have dressed for the occasion in his presence. The sight of the gun, a real gun and real cartridges, had scared him stiff. If he ran out on us now and we had to advertise again to find a new one—my God, I had just handed him a hundred bucks!

"Listen," I told him earnestly, "you said a minute ago that you expect nothing to happen. You may be right. I'm inclined to agree with you. But in case somebody does undertake to perform, I am wearing this little number"—I patted under my arm where the gun was—"for two purposes: first, to keep you from getting hurt; and second, if you do get hurt, to hurt him worse."

It seemed to satisfy him, for his eyes got less concentrated, but he didn't resume with the ginger snaps. At least I had accomplished that much. Using a matter-of-fact tone, which I thought would reassure him, I explained that he was to go to Wolfe's room at eleven-thirty for instructions, which would include our afternoon outing.

To tell the truth, by the time the afternoon was over and I had him back in the house again, a little after five-thirty, I had to maintain a firm hold on such details as ginger snaps and his calling me Archie to keep from admiring him. During that extended expedition we made stops at Brooks Brothers, Rusterman's, the Churchill, the Metropolitan Museum of Art, the Botanical Gardens, and three or four others. He occupied the rear seat, of course, because Wolfe always did, and the mirror showed me that he sat back comfortably, taking in the sights, a lot more imperturbable than Wolfe himself would have been, since Wolfe disliked motion, detested bumps, and had a settled notion that all the other cars had turned out for the express purpose of colliding with his.

When we made one of our stops and Hackett got out to cross the sidewalk, he was okay. He didn't hurry or dodge or jerk or weave, but just walked. In Wolfe's hat and coat and stick, he might even have fooled me. I had to hand it to him, in spite of the fact that the whole show struck me as the biggest bust Wolfe had ever concocted. At night it might be different, but there in broad daylight, and with no discernible evidence that anyone was on our trail, I felt foolish, futile, and fatuous, and still I had to keep alert, covering all directions, with the gun in my hand resting on the seat.

Nothing happened. Not a damn thing.

Back at the house, I left Hackett in the office and went to the kitchen, where Wolfe was sitting at the big table drinking beer and watching Fritz make tomato juice. His daily routine was of course all shot.

I reported, "They tried to get him from the top of the Palisades with a howitzer, but missed him. He has a little bruise on his left elbow from the revolving door at Rusterman's, but otherwise unhurt."

Wolfe grunted. "How did he behave?"

"Okay."

Wolfe grunted again. "After dark we may more reasonably expect results. I repeat what I told you at noon: you will take an active part in the interview with Miss Geer, but you will restrain yourself. If you permit yourself to get fanciful, there is no telling what the effect may be on Mr. Hackett. As you know, his instructions are precise, but his discipline is questionable. See that she speaks up, so I can hear her. Seat her at the corner of my desk farthest from you so I will have a good view of her. The view through that hole is restricted."

"Yes, sir."

But as it turned out, I wasn't able to obey orders. It was then nearly six o'clock. When the doorbell rang a few minutes later and I went to answer it, glancing in at the office on my way down the hall to make sure that Hackett didn't have his feet up on the desk, I opened the door to find that Miss Geer hadn't ventured alone on the streets of the great city after all. Major Emil Jensen was there with her.

VI

I had the door open. It wouldn't have been courteous to slam it shut again and leave them on the stoop while I considered matters, so I dallied on the doorsill.

"Well," I said brightly, "two on one hook?"

Jensen said hello. Jane said, "You couldn't have had that thought up, because Major Jensen decided to come on the spur of the moment. We were having cocktails." She looked me up and down; it was true that I was sort of blocking the way and not moving. "May we come in?"

Certainly I could have told Jensen we only had one extra chair so he had better go for a walk, but if there was going to be anything accomplished by having either of those two get the idea that Hackett was Nero Wolfe, I would have picked him for the experiment rather than her. On the other hand, with Hackett primed only for her it would have been crowding our luck to confront him with both of them; and anyway, I couldn't take such a chance on my own hook. I needed advice from headquarters. So I decided to herd them into the front room, and ask them to wait, and go to consult Wolfe.

"Sure," I said hospitably, "enter." I gave them gangway, and when they were in, shut the door and opened the door to the front room. "In there, please. Find seats. If you don't mind waiting a minute—"

I had got myself headed back for the hall before noticing an unfortunate fact: the door from the front room to the office was standing open. That was careless of me, but I hadn't expected complications. If they moved across, as they naturally would, Hackett sitting in the office would be in plain sight. But what the hell, that was what he was there for. So I kept going, down the hall to the turn into the alcove at the far end, found Wolfe there ready to take position at the peep-hole, and muttered to him:

"She brought an outrider along. Major Jensen. I put them in the front room. The door into the office is open. Well?"

He scowled at me. He whispered, "Confound it. Return to the front room by way of the office, closing that door as you go. Tell Major Jensen to wait, that I wish to speak with Miss Geer privately. Take her to the office by way of the hall, and when you—"

Somebody fired a gun.

At least that's what it sounded like, and the sound didn't come from outdoors. The walls and the air vibrated. Judging by the noise, I might have fired it myself, but I hadn't. I moved. In three jumps I was at the door to the office. Hackett was sitting there, looking startled and speechless. I dashed through to the front room. Jensen and Jane were there, on their feet, she off to the right and he to the left, both also startled and speechless, staring at each other. Their hands were empty, except for Jane's bag. I might have been inclined to let it go for Hackett biting a ginger snap if it hadn't been for the smell. I knew that smell.

I snapped at Jensen, "Well?"

"Well yourself." He had transferred the stare to me. "What the hell was it?"

"Did you fire a gun?"

"No. Did you?"

I pivoted to Jane. "Did you?"

"You—you idiot," she stammered. She was trying not to tremble. "Why would I fire a gun?"

"Let me see that one in your hand," Jensen demanded.

I looked at my hand and was surprised to see a gun in it. I must have snatched it from the holster automatically en route. "Not it," I said. I poked the muzzle to within an inch of Jensen's nose. "Was it?"

He sniffed. "No." He felt the barrel, found it cold, and shook his head.

I said, "But a gun was fired inside here. Do you smell it?"

"Certainly I smell it."

"Okay. Let's join Mr. Wolfe and discuss it. Through there." I indicated the door to the office with a flourish of the gun.

Jane started jabbering, but I paid no attention. She was merely jabbering, something indignant about a put-up job and so on. She was disinclined to enter the office, but when Jensen went she followed him and I brought up the rear.

"This is Mr. Nero Wolfe," I said. "Sit down," I was using my best judgment and figured I was playing it right because Wolfe was nowhere in sight. I had to decide what to do with them while I found the gun and maybe the bullet. Jane was still trying to jabber, but she stopped when Jensen blurted, "Wolfe has blood on his head!"

I stared at Hackett. He was standing up behind the desk, leaning forward with his hand resting on the desk, looking the three of us over with an expression that left it open whether he was dazed, scared, or angry, or all three. He didn't seem to hear Jensen's words. When I did I saw the blood on Hackett's left ear and dribbling down the side of his neck.

I took in breath and yelled, "Fritz!"

He appeared instantly, probably having been standing by in the hall by Wolfe's direction. I told him to come here, and when he came handed him my gun. "If anybody reaches for a handkerchief, shoot."

"Those instructions," Jensen said sharply, "are dangerous if he—"

"He's all right."

"I would like you to search me." Jensen stuck his hands toward the ceiling.

"That," I said, "is more like it," and crossed to him and explored him from neck to ankles, invited him to relax in a chair, and turned to Jane. She darted me a look of pure and lofty disgust and backed away as from a noxious miasma.

I remarked, "If you refuse to stand inspection and then you happen to make a gesture and Fritz shoots you in the tummy, don't blame me."

She darted more looks, but took it. I felt her over not quite as comprehensively as I had Jensen, took her bag and glanced in it and returned it to her, and then stepped around Wolfe's desk to examine Hackett's blood. He wasn't screaming or moaning, but the expression on his face was something. After Jensen had announced the blood, he had put his hand up to feel, and he was staring at the red on his fingers with his big jaw hanging open.

"My head?" he croaked. "Is it my head?"

The exhibition he was making of himself was no help to Nero Wolfe's reputation for intrepidity. After a brief look I told him distinctly, "No, sir. Nothing but a nick in the upper outside corner of your ear." I wiped with my handkerchief. "You might go to the bathroom and use a towel."

"I am not—hurt?"

I could have murdered him. Instead, I told Fritz, standing there with my gun, that unnecessary movements were still forbidden, and took Hackett to the bathroom in the far corner and shut the door behind me. While I showed him the ear in the mirror and dabbed on some iodine and taped on a bandage, I told him to stay in there until his nerves calmed down and then rejoin us, act detached and superior, and let me do the talking. He said he would, but at that moment I would have traded him for one wet cigarette.

As I reappeared in the office, Jane shot at me, "Did you search him?" I ignored her and circled around Wolfe's desk for a look at the back of the chair. The head-rest was upholstered in brown leather; and about eight inches from the top and a foot from the side edge, a spot that would naturally have been on a line behind Hackett's left ear as he sat, there was a hole in the leather. I looked behind, and there was another hole on the rear side. I looked at the wall back of the chair and found still another hole, torn into the plaster. From the bottom drawer of my desk I got a screwdriver and hammer, started chiseling, ran against a stud, and went to work with the point of my knife. When I finally turned around I held a small object between my thumb and finger. As I did so Hackett emerged from the bathroom, apparently more composed.

"Bullet," I said informatively. "Thirty-eight. Passed through Mr. Wolfe's ear and the back of his chair and ruined the wall. Patched plaster is an eyesore."

Jane sputtered. Jensen sat and gazed at me with narrowed eyes. Hackett said, in what he probably thought was a detached and superior tone, "I'll search them again." I tried not to glare at him.

"No, sir," I said deferentially, "I made sure of that. But I suggest—"

"It could be," Jensen put in, "that Wolfe fired that bullet himself."

"Yeah?" I returned his gaze. "Mr. Wolfe would be glad to let you inspect his face for powder marks."

"He washed them off in the bathroom," Jane snapped.

"They don't wash off." I continued to Jensen, "I'll lend you a magnifying glass. You can examine the leather on the chair too."

By gum, he took me up. He nodded and arose, and I got the glass from Wolfe's desk, the big one. First he went over the chair, the portion in the neighborhood of the bullet hole, and then crossed to Hackett and gave his face and ear a look. Hackett stood still, with his lips compressed and his eyes straight ahead. Jensen gave me back the glass and returned to his seat.

I asked him, "Did Mr. Wolfe shoot himself in the ear?"

"No," he admitted. "Not unless he had the gun wrapped."

"Sure." My tone cut slices off of them. "He tied a pillow around it, held it at arm's length, pointing it at his ear, and pulled the trigger. How would you like to try demonstrating it? Keeping the bullet within an inch of your frontal lobe?"

He never stopped gazing at me. "I am," he declared, "being completely objective. With some difficulty. I agree it is highly improbable."

"If I understand what happened—" Hackett began, but I doubted if he was going to offer anything useful, so I cut him off.

"Excuse me, sir. The bullet helps, but the gun would help still more. Let's be objective too. We might possibly find the object in the front room." I moved, touching his elbow to take him along. "Fritz, see that they stay put."

"I," said Jensen, getting up, "would like to be present—"

"The hell you would." I wheeled to him. My voice may have gone up a notch. "Sit down, brother. I am trying not to fly off the handle. I am trying not to be rude. Whose house is this, with bullets zipping around? I swear to God Fritz will shoot you in the knee."

He had another remark to contribute, and so did Jane, but I disregarded them and wrangled Hackett ahead of me into the front room and shut the soundproof door. Hackett began to talk, but I shut him off. He insisted he had something to say. I told him to spill it.

"It seems incredible," he asserted, meeting my eye and choosing his words, "that one of them could have shot at me from in here, through the open door, without me seeing anything."

"You said that before, in the bathroom. You also said you didn't remember whether your eyes were open or shut, or where you were looking, when you heard that shot." I moved my face to within fourteen inches of his. "See here. If you are suspecting that I shot at you, or that Wolfe did, you have got fleas or other insects playing tag in your brain and should have it attended to. One thing alone: the way the bullet went, straight past your ear and into the chair back, it had to come from in front, the general direction of that door and this room. It couldn't have come from the door in the hall or anywhere else, because we haven't got a gun that

100

shoots a curve. I can't help it if your eyes were focused somewhere else or were closed or you went temporarily blind. You will please sit in that chair against the wall and not move or talk."

He grumbled but obeyed. I surveyed the field. On the assumption that the gun had been fired in that room, I adopted the theory that either it was still there or it had been transported or propelled without. As for transportation, I had got there not more than five seconds after the shot and found them there staring at each other. As for propulsion, the windows were closed and the venetian blinds down. I preferred the first alternative and began to search.

Obviously it couldn't be anything abstruse, since five seconds wasn't long enough to pry up a floor board or make a hole in a table leg, so I tried easier places, like under furniture and behind cushions. It might be thought that under the circumstances I would have been dead sure of finding it, but I had the curious feeling that I probably wouldn't no matter how thoroughly I looked; I have never understood why. If it was a hunch it was a bad day for hunches, because when I came to the big vase on the table between the windows and peeked into it and saw something white and stuck my hand in, I felt the gun. Getting it by the trigger guard, I lifted it out. Judging by smell, it had been fired recently, but of course it had had time to cool off. It was an old Granville thirty-eight, next door to rusty. The white object I had seen was an ordinary cotton handkerchief, man's size, with a tear in it through which the butt of the gun protruded. With proper care about touching, I opened the cylinder and found there were five loaded cartridges and one shell.

Hackett was there beside me, trying to say things. I got brusque with him.

"Yes, it's a gun, recently fired, and not mine or Wolfe's. Is it yours? No? Good. Okay, keep your shirt on. We're going back in there, and there will be sufficient employment for my brain without interference from you. Do not try to help me. See how long you can go without speaking a word. Just look wise as if you knew it all. If this ends as it ought to, you'll get an extra hundred. Agreed?"

I'll be damned if he didn't say, "Two hundred. I was shot at. I came within an inch of getting killed."

I told him he'd have to talk the second hundred out of Wolfe and opened the door to the office and followed him through. He detoured around Jane Geer and went and sat in the chair he had just escaped being a corpse in. I swiveled my own chair to face it out and sat down too.

Jensen demanded sharply, "What have you got there?"

"This," I said cheerfully, "is a veteran revolver, a Granville thirty-eight, which has been fired not too long ago." I lowered it gently onto my desk. "Fritz, give me back my gun." He brought it. I kept it in my hand. "Thank you. I found this other affair in the vase on the table in there, dressed in a handkerchief. Five unused cartridges and one used. It's a stranger here. Never saw it before. It appears to put the finishing touch on a critical situation."

Jane exploded. She called me an unspeakable rat. She said she wanted a lawyer and intended to go to one immediately. She called Hackett three or four things. She said it was the dirtiest frame-up in history. "Now," she told Hackett, "I know damned well you framed Peter Root. I let that skunk Goodwin talk me out of it!" She was out of her chair, spitting fire. It was spectacular. "You won't get away with it this time! You incredible louse!"

Hackett was trying to talk back to her, making his voice louder and louder, and when she stopped for breath he could be heard.

". . . will not tolerate it! You come here and try to kill me! You nearly do kill me! Then you abuse me about a Peter Root and I have never heard of Peter Root!" He was putting real feeling into it; apparently he had either forgotten that he was supposed to be Nero Wolfe, or had got the notion, in all the excitement, that he really was Nero Wolfe. He was proceeding, "Young lady, listen to me! I will not—"

She turned and made for the door. I was immediately on my feet and after her, but halfway across the room I put on the brake, because the doorway had suddenly filled up with a self-propelled massive substance

102

and she couldn't get through. She stopped, goggle-eyed, and then fell back a couple of paces. The massive substance advanced, halted, and used its mouth.

"How do you do. I am Nero Wolfe."

VII

He did it well, at top form, and it was quite an effect.

Nobody made a chirp. He moved forward, and Jane retreated again, moving backwards without looking around and nearly tripping on Jensen's feet. Wolfe stopped at the corner of his desk and wiggled a finger at Hackett.

"Take another chair, sir, if you please?"

Hackett sidled out, without a word, and went to the red leather chair. Wolfe leaned over to peer at the hole in the back of his own chair, and then at the hole in the plaster, which I had chiseled to a diameter of four inches, grunted, and got himself seated.

"This," Jensen said, "makes it a farce."

Jane snapped, "I'm going," and headed for the door, but I had been expecting that and with only two steps had her by the arm with a good grip and was prepared to give her the twist if she went thorny on me. Jensen sprang to his feet, with both of his hands fists. Evidently in the brief space of forty-eight hours it had developed to the point where the sight of another man lying hands on his Jane started his adrenalin spurting in torrents. If he had come close enough to make it necessary to slap him with my free hand he might have got blood on his ear too, because I had my gun in that hand.

"Stop it!" Wolfe's voice was a whip. It turned us into a group of statuary. "Miss Geer, you may leave shortly, if you still want to, after I have said something. Mr. Jensen, sit down. Mr. Goodwin has a gun and is probably in a temper, and might hurt you. Archie, go to your desk, but be ready to use the gun. One of them is a murderer."

"That's a lie!" Jensen was visibly breathing. "And who the hell are you?"

"I introduced myself, sir. That gentleman is my temporary employee. When my life was threatened I hired him to impersonate me. If I had known the worst to be expected was a gash in the ear I could have saved some money and spared myself a vast amount of irritation."

Jane spat at him, "You fat coward!"

He shook his head. "No, Miss Geer. It is no great distinction not to be a coward, but I can claim it. Not cowardice. Conceit. I am insufferably conceited. I was convinced that the person who killed Mr. Jensen would be equally daring, witty, and effective in dealing with me. Should I be killed, I doubted if the murderer would ever be caught. Should another be killed in my place, I would still be alive to attend to the matter myself. Justified conceit, but still conceit." He turned abruptly to me. "Archie, get Inspector Cramer on the phone."

They both started talking at once, with vehemence. I watched them from a corner of an eye while dialing. Wolfe cut them off.

"If you please! In a moment I shall offer you an alternative: the police or me. Meanwhile Mr. Cramer can help. One of you, of course, is putting all this on; to the other I wish to say that you might as well sit down and resign yourself to some inconvenience and unpleasantness." He glanced at Hackett. "It you want to get away from this uproar, there is your room upstairs . . ."

"I think I'll stay here," Hackett declared. "I'm a little interested in this myself, since I nearly got killed."

"Cramer on," I told Wolfe.

He lifted his phone from the cradle. "How do you do, sir. No. No, I have a request to make. If you send a man here right away, I'll give him a revolver and a bullet. First, examine the revolver for fingerprints and send me copies. Second, trace the revolver if possible. Third, fire a bullet from it and compare it both with the bullet I am sending you and with the bullets that killed Mr. Jensen and Mr. Doyle. Let me know the results. That's all. No. Confound it, no! If you come yourself you will be handed the package at the door and not admitted. I'm busy."

As he hung up I said, "The number has been filed off the gun."

"Then it can't be traced."

"No, sir. Does Cramer get the handkerchief too?"

"Let me see it."

I handed the gun to him, with its butt still protruding through the tear in the handkerchief. Wolfe frowned as he saw that the handkerchief had no laundry mark or any other mark and was a species that could be bought in at least a thousand stores in New York City alone, not to mention the rest of the country.

"We'll keep the handkerchief," Wolfe said.

Jensen demanded, "What the devil is it doing there?"

Wolfe's eyes went shut. He was, of course, tasting Jensen's expression, tone of voice, and mental longitude and latitude, to try to decide whether innocent curiosity was indicated or a camouflage for guilt. He always shut his eyes when he tasted. In a moment they opened again halfway.

"If a man has recently shot a gun," he said, "and has had no opportunity to wash, an examination of his hand will furnish incontestable proof. You probably know that. One of you, the one who fired that shot, certainly does. The handkerchief protected the hand. Under a microscope it would be found to contain many minute particles of explosive and other residue. The fact that it is a man's handkerchief doesn't help. Major Jensen would naturally possess a man's handkerchief. If Miss Geer decided to use a handkerchief in that manner, naturally she wouldn't use a woman's handkerchief. Anyway, it wouldn't be big enough."

"You asked me to stay while you said something," Jane snapped. She and Jensen were back in their chairs. "You haven't said anything yet. Where were *you* when the shot was fired?"

"Pfui." Wolfe sighed. "Fritz, pack the gun and bullet in a carton, carefully with tissue paper, and give it to the man when he comes. First bring me beer. Do any of you want beer?"

Evidently no one did.

"Very well. Miss Geer. To assume, or pretend to assume some elaborate hocus-pocus by the inmates of this house is inane. At the moment the shot was fired I was standing near the kitchen talking with Mr. Goodwin. Since then I have been at a spot from which part of this room can be seen and voices heard."

His eyes went to Jensen and back to Jane. "One of you two people is apt to make a mistake, and I want to prevent it if possible. I have not yet asked you where you were and what you were doing at the instant the shot was fired. Before I do so I want to say this, that even with the information at hand it is demonstrable that the shot came from the direction of that door to the front room, which was standing open. Mr. Hackett could not have fired it; you, Mr. Jensen, satisfied yourself of that. Mr. Brenner was in the kitchen. Mr. Goodwin and I were together. I warn you—one of you—that this is sufficiently provable to satisfy a jury in a murder trial. Now what if you both assert that at the instant you heard the shot you were together, close together perhaps, looking at each other? For the one who fired the gun that would be a blessing indeed. For the other it might be disastrous in the end; for when the truth is disclosed, as it will be, the question of complicity will arise. How long have you two known each other?"

He knew; I had told him. But apparently they had both forgotten, for neither answered.

"Well?" Wolfe was crisp. "Miss Geer, how long have you been acquainted with Mr. Jensen. I don't suppose it's a secret?"

Jane's teeth were holding her lower lip. She removed them. "I met him day before yesterday. Here."

"Indeed. Is that correct, Mr. Jensen?"

"Yes."

Wolfe's brows were up. "Hardly long enough to form an attachment to warrant any of the more costly forms of sacrifice. Unless the spark was exceptionally hot, not long enough to weld you into collusion for murder. I hope you understand, Miss Geer, that all that is wanted here is the truth. Where were you and what were you doing when you heard the shot?"

"I was standing by the piano. I had put my bag on the piano and was opening it."

"Which way were you facing?"

"Toward the window."

"Were you looking at Mr. Jensen?"

"Not at that moment, no."

"Thank you." Wolfe's eyes moved. "Mr. Jensen?"

"I still say," Jensen said, "that it's a damned farce."

"Even so, sir, you're one of the cast. Surely it is risking little to tell me where—"

"I was in the doorway to the hall, looking down the hall and wondering where Goodwin had gone to. For no particular reason. I was not at that precise moment looking at Miss Geer. But I regard it as—"

"That won't help me any. How you regard it. And I doubt if it will help you." Wolfe poured beer, which Fritz had brought. "Now we are ready to decide something." He took them both in. "Miss Geer, you said you wanted to go to a lawyer, heaven protect you. But it would not be sensible to permit either of you to walk out of here, to move and act at your own will and discretion. Since that bullet was intended for me, I reject the notion utterly. On the other hand, we can't proceed intelligently until I get a report from Mr. Cramer. There is time to be passed. You can—"

Jane got up. "I'm going."

"One moment. You can either pass it here, in company with Mr. Goodwin and his gun, or I can phone Mr. Cramer, giving him an outline of the situation, and he can send men to get you. Which do you prefer?"

Jane was doing slow motion toward the door. She didn't exactly take a step; it was more as if something was pulling her that way without her doing anything about it. I called to her without leaving my chair, "Listen, honey, I wouldn't shoot you for a nickel, but I can easy catch you before you get out the front door and this time I'll wrap you up good."

She flung at me: "Rat!"

Jensen was paying no attention to us. His eyes stuck to Wolfe. He asked, not with any venom, just asking, "Which do *you* prefer?" Evidently he had decided to give us an exhibition of self-control.

Wolfe returned his gaze. "I should think," he said dryly, "that you would rather stay here. As you probably know, Mr. Cramer is not fond of you, and he is somewhat heavy-handed. Not that he can be kept out of it indefinitely, but the immediate question is where do you want to wait for the report on the gun and bullets, here or at police headquarters? It is likely to be several hours. I suggest that you will be more comfortable here." Wolfe glanced at the clock; it said twenty to seven. "There will of course be something to eat."

Jensen said, "I want to use the phone."

Wolfe shook his head. "No, sir. Shall I call Mr. Cramer?"

"No."

"Good. That's sensible. Miss Geer?"

She wasn't conversing. Wolfe waited patiently for four seconds.

"Shall I phone the police, Miss Geer?"

Her head went from side to side in a negative, the way she had moved toward the door, as if someone or something was doing it for her.

Wolfe heaved a sigh. "Archie, take them to the front room and stay there till I send for you. Fritz will answer the bell. I am aware that it will be tiresome, but there's no help for it."

VIII

Yes, it got tiresome, lasting as it did a full two hours.

At first I got some diversion out of the fact that Jane and Jensen showed no inclination to sit side by side on the sofa and hold hands. God knows where Wolfe had ever found that sofa and the velvet cushions; it had been there when I had first arrived. One or the other of them did sit on it now and again during their restless moving around, but not the two together. Wolfe's poison had done its work. It was interesting to watch it. The one who had not fired the gun had got suspicious of the other one; and the other one, seeing that, obviously had figured that if he or she tried to be cordial on the basis of what the hell, darling, we couldn't be murderers, could we, it would be a giveaway, because the one would be thinking, If I'm suspicious why isn't he or she?

Naturally I watched for something, any kind of sign, from which I could get a notion who was the one and who was the other, but now I leaned one way and now the other, and got nowhere.

At seven-thirty we were all invited to the dining-room, but they wouldn't go. When Fritz brought trays in to us I had no trouble dealing with my share of melon, broiled pork loin wafers, salad with Wolfe's own dressing, blueberry pie, and coffee, and Jensen was with me nose and nose, but Jane wouldn't even look at hers.

I was, I admit, in no condition to place a bet, even to risk as much as a busted shoestring. The only way I could have solved the problem would have been to blindfold myself and whichever one I touched first was it. Anyway, I was licked before I started, because bold and daring, which were words Wolfe had used, was putting it mildly. He or she had of course arrived at the house with the gun ready, dressed in the handkerchief, in pocket or handbag, but only with the idea of using it if opportunity offered, for it couldn't possibly have been planned just as it happened. For split-second decision and action I had never seen anything to equal it. Entered the room. Saw, through the open door, Wolfe (supposedly) seated at his desk. Got hand on gun, protected by handkerchief. Waited. Instant came, in about a minute, when Wolfe's eyes were closed or he was looking elsewhere, and also, simultaneously, the other one was either looking in the hall or was at the piano with back turned, depending on who was who. Aimed and fired. When the other one glanced in all directions, that provided the chance to put the gun in the vase.

The devil of it was, try to crack it. Unless you could make it fairly overwhelming by way of motive or possession of the gun or something else from the build-up, how were you going to get a jury to convict either of them? Not to mention the little item that what was really wanted was conviction not for felonious assault on Hackett, but for the murder of Jensen and Doyle.

During the two hours I spoke to Jane three times, at well-spaced intervals, as follows:

1. "Do you want a drink of water or something?"
2. "There's a door to that bathroom from this room

too. Over there. The one from the bathroom to the office is now locked."

3. "I beg your pardon." That was for a yawn.

She neither spoke to me nor looked at me. Jensen was about as bad. I don't remember any two hours in my experience with a lower score on joviality.

So I appreciated the break in the monotony when, a little before nine, I heard the doorbell. Since the door from the front room to the hall was also soundproof, that was all I got out of it except for the faint vibration of footsteps and an even fainter sound of voices. But in about three minutes the door to the hall opened and Fritz came in. He shut the door behind him and spoke, not very loud.

"Archie, Mr. Wolfe wants you in the office. Inspector Cramer is there with Sergeant Stebbins. I am to stay here."

He held out his hand for the gun. I gave it to him and went.

If the situation in the front room had been unjovial, the one in the office was absolutely grim. One glance at Wolfe was enough to see that he was in a state of uncontrollable fury, because his forefinger was making the same circle, over and over, on the surface of his desk. Sergeant Purley Stebbins was standing by the wall, looking official. Inspector Cramer was in the red leather chair, with his face about the color of the chair. Nobody bothered to glance at me.

Wolfe snapped, "Your notebook."

I crossed to my desk and got book and pencil and sat down. "This," I observed, "is what comes of my not attending to the doorbell. If we didn't want company—"

"Pfui." Wolfe tapped a piece of paper on his desk. "Look at this."

I arose and looked. It was a search warrant. "The premises ... owned and inhabited by said Nero Wolfe ... situate ..."

Wowie. I was surprised that Cramer was still alive, or Wolfe either.

Cramer growled, holding himself in, "I'll try to forget what you just said, Wolfe. It was totally uncalled for. Goddam it, you have given me a runaround too many times. There I was, with that gun. A bullet fired from it matched the bullet you sent me and also the two that killed Jensen and Doyle. That's the gun, and you sent it to me. All right, then you've got a client, and when you've got a client you keep him right in your pocket. I would have been a goddam fool to come here and start begging you. I've begged you before."

Wolfe had started making the circle again. "I repeat, sir," he murmured, "that your acceptance of your salary constitutes a fraud on the people of New York and you are a disgrace to an honorable profession."

Cramer's face had reached the red of the chair and was going on from there. "Then," he said, "I won't try to forget it. We're going to search this house." He started to leave the chair.

"If you do you'll never catch the murderer of Mr. Jensen and Mr. Doyle."

Cramer dropped back in the chair. "I won't?"

"No, sir."

"You'll prevent me?"

"Bah." Wolfe was disgusted. "Next you'll be warning me formally that obstruction of justice is a crime. I didn't say that the murderer would be caught, I said you wouldn't catch him. Because I already have."

A grunt came from Purley Stebbins, but no one noticed it but me. I grinned at him.

Cramer said, "The hell you have."

"Yes, sir. Your report on the gun and bullets settles it. But I confess the matter is a little complicated, and I do give you a formal warning: you are not equipped to handle it. I am." Wolfe shoved the warrant across the desk. "Tear that thing up."

Cramer slowly shook his head. "You see, Wolfe, I know you. God, don't I know you! But I'm willing to have a talk before I execute it."

"No, sir." Wolfe was murmuring again. "I will not submit to duress. I would even prefer to deal with District Attorney Skinner. Tear it up, or proceed to execute it."

That was a dirty threat. Cramer's opinion of Skinner was one of the defects of our democratic system of government. Cramer looked at the warrant, at Wolfe, at me, and back at the warrant. Then he picked it up and tore. I reached for the pieces and dropped them in the wastebasket.

Wolfe didn't look gratified because he was still too sore to let any other emotion in, but he did quit murmuring and allowed himself to talk. "Confound it," he said. "Don't ever waste your time like that again. Or mine. Can the gun be traced?"

"No. The number's gone. It dates from about nineteen-ten. And there are no prints on it that are worth a damn. Nothing but smudges."

Wolfe nodded. "Naturally. A much simpler technique than wiping it clean or going around in gloves." He glanced at Stebbins. "Please sit down, sir. Your standing there annoys me." Back to Cramer. "The murderer is in this house."

"I suspect he was. Is he your client?"

Wolfe let that one go by without even waving at it. Leaning back in his chair, adjusting himself with accompanying grunts and interlacing his fingers at the Greenwich meridian on his equator, he was ready to forget the search warrant and get down to business. I winked at Purley, but he pretended not to see it. He had his notebook too, but hadn't put anything in it yet.

"The main complication," Wolfe said in his purring tone, "is this. There are a man and a woman in the front room. Granting that one of them is the murderer, which one?"

Cramer frowned at him. "You didn't say anything about granting. You said that you had caught the murderer."

"So I have. He or she is in there, under guard. I suppose I'll have to tell you what happened, if I expect you to start your army of men digging, and it looks as though that's the only way to go about it. I have no army. To begin with, when I received that threat I hired a man who resembles me—superficially—in physical characteristics to be visible, both in this house and on the street, and I kept to my room. Nothing occurred—"

"Not involved, not inter—"

"Please don't interrupt," Wolfe snapped. "I'm telling you what happened."

He did so. I have a high opinion of myself as a reporter of a series of events, but, listening to Wolfe as an expert, I had to admit I couldn't have done much better. He didn't waste any words, but he got it all in. Purley nearly bit the end of his tongue off, trying to get it all in his notebook, but I didn't bother.

Wolfe finished. Cramer sat scowling. Wolfe purred, "Well, sir, there's the problem. I doubt if it can be solved with what we have, or what is available on the premises. You'll have to get your men started on the indicated lines. I'll be available for consultation."

"I wish," Cramer growled, gazing at him as if he were looking at a puzzle he had seen and worked at many times but had never got it solved, "I wish I knew how much dressing you put on that."

"Not any. I have only one concern in this. I have no client. I withheld nothing and added nothing."

"Maybe." Cramer straightened up like a man of action. "Okay, we'll proceed on that basis and find out. First of all, I want to ask them some questions."

"I suppose you do." Wolfe detested sitting and listening to someone else ask questions, especially in his own office. "And Miss Geer is going to be difficult. She wants a lawyer. You are handicapped, of course, by your official status. Which one do you want first?"

Cramer stood up. "I've got to see that room before I talk to either of them. I want to see where things are. Especially that vase."

I was amazed to see that Wolfe was leaving his chair too, knowing his attitude toward all non-essential movement, but as I went to open the door to the front room for them I reflected that while he hated hearing Cramer ask questions, under the circumstances he would hate even more not hearing him, in case conversation got started in the front room. Stebbins tagged in after them, and I brought up the rear.

Jane was seated on the piano bench. Jensen was on the sofa, but arose as we entered. Fritz was standing by a window, his hand with the gun coming up as Jensen moved.

Wolfe said, "This is Inspector Cramer, Miss Geer."

She didn't make a sound or move a muscle.

Wolfe said, "I believe you've met the inspector, Mr. Jensen."

113

"Yes, I have." Jensen's voice had gone unused so long it squeaked, and he cleared his throat. "So the agreement not to call in the police was a farce too." He was bitter.

"There was no such agreement. I said that Mr. Cramer couldn't be kept out of it indefinitely. The bullet that was fired at me—at Mr. Hackett—came from the gun that was found in that vase"—Wolfe pointed at it—"and so did those that killed your father and Mr. Doyle. So the field has become—ah, restricted."

"I insist," Jane put in, in a voice with no resemblance to any I had ever heard her use before, "on my right to consult a lawyer."

"Just a minute now," Cramer told her in the tone he thought was soothing. "We're going to talk this over, but wait till I look around a little." He proceeded to inspect things, and so did Sergeant Stebbins. They considered distances, and the positions of various objects. Then there was this detail: from what segment of that room could a gun send a bullet through the open door to the office and on through the hole in Wolfe's chair and the one in the wall?

They were working on that together when Wolfe turned to Fritz and asked him, "What happened to the other cushion?"

Fritz was taken aback. "Other cushion?"

"There were six velvet cushions on that sofa. There are only five. Did you remove it?"

"No, sir." Fritz gazed at the sofa and counted. "That's right. They've been rearranged to take up the space. I don't understand it. They were all here yesterday when I cleaned in here."

"Are you sure of that?"

"Yes, sir. Positive."

"Look for it. Archie, help him. I want to know if that cushion is in this room."

It seemed like an odd moment to send out a general alarm for a sofa cushion, but since I had nothing else to do at the moment I obliged. Cramer and Purley went on solving a murder and Fritz and I went on hunting the cushion. Jensen watched both operations. Wolfe watched only one—Fritz's and mine. Jane pretended there was no one in the room but her.

114

I finally told Wolfe, "It's gone. It isn't in here."

He muttered at me, "I see it isn't."

I stared at him. There was an expression on his face that I knew well. It wasn't exactly excitement, though it always stirred excitement in me. His neck was rigid, as if to prevent any movement of the head, so as not to disturb the brain, his eyes were half shut and not seeing anything, and his lips were moving, pushing out, then relaxing, then pushing out again. I knew it would take more than the loss of a velvet cushion to produce that effect on him. I stared at him.

Suddenly he turned and spoke. "Mr. Cramer! Please leave Mr. Stebbins in here with Miss Geer and Mr. Jensen. You can stay here too, or come with me, as you prefer. Fritz and Archie, come." He headed for the office.

Cramer, knowing Wolfe's tones of voice almost as well as I did, spoke to Stebbins and then followed. Fritz and I also followed. So did Jane's voice.

"This is outrageous! I want—"

I shut the door.

Wolfe waited until he was in his chair before he spoke. "I want to know if that cushion is on the premises. Search the house from the cellar up—except the south room; Mr. Hackett is in there lying down. Start in here."

Cramer barked, "What the hell is all this about?"

"I'll give you an explanation," Wolfe told him, "when I have one. I'm going to sit here and work and must not be disturbed. It may take ten minutes; it may take ten hours. Go in there; stay here; go anywhere, but let me alone."

He leaned back and closed his eyes, and his lips started moving. Cramer slid farther back in his chair, crossed his legs, got out a cigar and sank his teeth in it.

Searching the office was quite different from searching the front room. In the first place, it was a lot bigger. Also, there were a lot more places where you could hide a cushion—files, drawers, bookshelves, magazine and newspaper racks, cabinets, miscellaneous. It had a high ceiling, and the steps had to be used for all the upper shelves and file and cabinet compartments. None of them could be ruled out, because the shelves were deep, and it was no trivial job to pull out all those books and slide them back again. Fritz went at it with his usual deliberate thoroughness, and I couldn't have been called a whirlwind either because I was using my brain along with my hands, trying to work out how and why the fact of a missing cushion crashed into the structure like a comet shattering a world. Now and then a glance at Wolfe showed me that he was still working, his lips moving and his eyes shut.

Half an hour or so had passed, maybe a little more, when I heard him let out a grunt. I nearly toppled off the steps, turning to look at him. He was in motion. He picked up his wastebasket, which was kept at the far corner of his desk, held it so that the light shone directly into it, inspected it, shook his head, put it down again, and began opening the drawers of his desk, all the way out, and inspecting their interiors, starting with the top one on the right side. The first two, the one at the top and the one in the middle apparently didn't get him anything, but when he yanked out the double-depth one at the bottom as far as it would go, he looked in, bent over closer to see better, stuck a hand in and seemed to be poking around, closed the drawer, got himself erect, and announced:

"I've found it."

In those three little words there was at least two tons of self-satisfaction and smirk.

We all goggled at him.

He looked at me. "Archie. Get down off that thing and don't fall. Look in your desk and see if one of my guns has been fired."

I stepped down and went and opened the armament drawer. The first one I picked up was innocent. I tried the second with a sniff and a look and reported, "Yes, sir. There were six cartridges and now there are five. Same as the cushions. The shell is here."

"Tchah! The confounded ass! Tell Miss Geer and Mr. Jensen that they may come in here if they care to hear what happened, or they may go home or anywhere else. We don't need them. Take Mr. Stebbins upstairs with you and bring Mr. Hackett down here. Use caution and search him with great care. He is an extremely dangerous man and an unsurpassable idiot."

IX

I had no hand in the phone call to General Fife—or rather, as I learned later, to Colonel Voss, who was on duty that evening at the downtown G-2 headquarters—because I was busy with the chores. First, with regard to Jane and Jensen. When I delivered Wolfe's message to them, in a few well-chosen words, they blinked in bewilderment, which was understandable. Then they both opened the valves and here came the steam. I silenced them by mere force of personality.

I told Jensen, "You came to see Wolfe to get him to help catch the murderer of your father. He has not only helped, he has done it singlehanded, practically without getting out of bed. For God's sake, what more do you want?"

I told Jane, "You wanted to avoid publicity as a suspect in a murder case so you can be a vice-president. Wolfe has done the avoiding for you. As my contribution, I have made you acquainted with this prominent major. You should beef?"

Naturally they voted for joining the throng in the office, and their pose during the balloting was significant. They stood facing each other, with Jensen's right hand on Jane's left shoulder, and Jane's right hand, or perhaps just the fingers, on Jensen's left forearm. I left it to them to find the way to the office alone, told Purley Stebbins what our job was, and took him upstairs with me to the south room.

It was approximately ten minutes later that we delivered our cargo in the office. Even though Mr. Hackett staged one of the most convincing demonstrations of unwillingness to cooperate that I have ever encountered, beginning the instant I put a hand on him to frisk him, only about six of the ten minutes were devoted to persuading him that there were worse things than going downstairs. For the other four minutes I sat on him, examining my shin to see if his kicks had busted the skin and testing my wrist to decide if it was sprained, while Purley was in the bathroom washing blood off his cheek and neck and applying Band-Aids.

Not that Hackett had confined himself to kicking and scratching; he hadn't confined himself at all. Purley and I did the confining.

We got him to the office in one piece, nothing really wrong with him but a few bruises, and put him in a chair. Purley took an upright position right behind him, with the evident intention of standing by, so I went to my desk. Jane and Jensen were on a couple of chairs side by side, over near the big globe. Cramer was as before.

I said, "He was reluctant."

I'll say one thing for Wolfe, I've never seen him gloat over a guy about to get it. He was contemplating Hackett more as an extraordinary object that deserved study.

I said, "Purley thinks he knows him."

Purley, as was proper, spoke to his superior. "I swear, Inspector, I'm sure I've seen him somewhere, but I can't remember."

Wolfe nodded. "A uniform makes a difference. I suggest that he was in uniform."

"Uniform?" Purley scowled. "Army?"

Wolfe shook his head. "Mr. Cramer told me Wednesday morning that the doorman on duty at the apartment house at the time Mr. Jensen and Mr. Doyle were killed was a fat nitwit who had been hired two weeks ago and didn't know the tenants by name, and also that he claimed to have been in the basement stoking the water heater at the moment the murders were committed. A phone call would tell us whether he is still working there."

"He isn't," Cramer growled. "He left Wednesday afternoon because he didn't like a place where people got murdered. I never saw him. Some of my men did."

"Yeah," Purley said, gazing at Hackett's face. "By God, it's him. I thought he didn't have brains enough to know which end to pick up a shovel."

"He is," Wolfe declared, "a remarkable combination of fool and genius. He came to New York determined to kill Mr. Jensen and me. By the way, Mr. Hackett, you look a little dazed. Can you hear what I'm saying?"

Hackett made no sound and didn't flutter an eyelid.

118

"I guess you can," Wolfe went on. "This will interest you. I requested Military Intelligence to have an examination made of the effects of Captain Peter Root at the prison in Maryland. A few minutes ago I phoned for a report, and got it. Captain Root was lying when he stated that he was not in communication with his father and had not been for years. There are several letters from his father among his belongings, dated in the past two months, and they make it evident that his father, whose name is Thomas Root, regards him as a scion to be proud of. To the point of mania." Wolfe wiggled a finger at Hackett. "I offer the conjecture that you are in a position to know whether that is correct or not. Is it?"

"One more day," Hackett said in his husky croak. His hands were twitching. "One more day," he repeated.

Wolfe nodded. "I know. One more day and you would have killed me, with the suspicion centered on Miss Geer or Mr. Jensen, or both, on account of your flummery here this afternoon. And you would have disappeared, probably after again complaining that you don't like a place where people get murdered."

Jensen popped up, "You haven't explained the flummery."

"I shall, Mr. Jensen." Wolfe got more comfortable in his chair. "But first that performance Tuesday evening." He was keeping his eyes on Hackett. "That was a masterpiece. You decided to kill Mr. Jensen first, which was lucky for me, and, since all apartment-house service staffs are short-handed, got a job there as doorman with no difficulty. All you had to do was await an opportunity, with no passers-by or other onlookers. It came the day after you mailed the threat, an ideal situation in every respect except the presence of the man he had hired to guard him. Arriving at the entrance to the apartment house, naturally they would have no suspicion of the doorman in uniform. Mr. Jensen probably nodded and spoke to you. With no one else in sight, and the elevator man ascending with a passenger, it was too good an opportunity to lose. Muffling the revolver with some piece of cloth, you shot Mr. Doyle in the back, and when Mr. Jensen whirled at the sound you shot him in the front and skedaddled for the stairs to the basement and started stoking the water heater. I imagine the first thing you fed it was the cloth with which you had muffled the gun."

Wolfe moved his eyes. "Does that rattle anywhere, Mr. Cramer?"

"It sounds tight from here," Cramer conceded.

"That's good. Because it is for those murders that Mr. Hackett—or Mr. Root, I suppose I should say—must be convicted. He can't be electrocuted for hacking a little gash in his own ear." Wolfe's eyes moved again, to me. "Archie, did you find any tools in his pockets?"

"Only a Boy Scout's dream," I told him. "One of those knives with scissors, awl, nail file . . ."

"Let the police have it to look for traces of blood. Just the sort of thing Mr. Cramer does best."

"The comedy can wait," Cramer growled. "I'll take it as is for Tuesday night and go on from there. What about today?"

Wolfe heaved a sigh. "You're rushing past the most interesting point of all: Mr. Hackett's answering my advertisement for a man. Was he sufficiently acute to realize that its specifications were roughly a description of me, suspect that I was the advertiser, and proceed to take advantage of it to approach me? Or was it merely that he was short of funds and attracted by the money offered? I lean to the latter, but I confess I am curious. I don't suppose, Mr. Root, you would care to clear that up for me?"

Mr. Root was not clearing up today.

"Very well. I can offer no inducement. In any event, having answered the advertisement and received a message from me, you were of course delighted, and doubly delighted when you were hired." Wolfe's eyes described an arc, including everybody in the roundup. "I invite comment, anything from irony to derision, on the fact that I paid a hundred dollars a day, to get him to live in my house, eat my food, and sit in my chair, to a man who had resolved to kill me. I can afford the invitation only because, in spite of that overwhelming handicap, I shall go on living and he will not."

Nobody seemed to have any irony or derision ready,

120

but Jensen chipped in, "You still haven't explained the flummery."

Wolfe nodded at him. "I'm getting to it, sir. Naturally, from the moment he got in here, Mr. Root was concocting schemes, rejecting, considering, revising; and no doubt relishing the situation enormously. The device of the handkerchief to protect a hand firing a gun was no doubt a part of one of those schemes, but it served admirably for the one he finally used. This morning he learned that Miss Geer was to call on me at six o'clock, and he was to impersonate me. After lunch, in here alone, he got a cushion from the sofa in there, wrapped his revolver in it, and fired a bullet through the back of this chair into the wall. He could, if he wished, have held the thing right against the back of the chair, and probably did. He stuffed the cushion into the rear compartment of the bottom right-hand drawer of this desk, having observed that the contents of the front of the drawer indicated that it was rarely opened. He put the gun in his pocket. He kept the chair pushed back to the wall to cover the hole in the plaster. The hole in the leather was not conspicuous and he took the risk of its being seen; when he was in the chair he covered the hole with his head."

"If the hole had been seen the bullet would have been found," Cramer muttered.

"I have already pronounced him," Wolfe said testily, "an unsurpassable fool. Even so, he knew that Archie would be out with him the rest of the afternoon, and I would be in my room. I had made a remark which informed him that I would not sit in that chair again until he was permanently out of it. At six o'clock Miss Geer arrived, unexpectedly accompanied by Mr. Jensen. They were shown into the front room, and that door was open. Mr. Root's brain moved swiftly, and so did the rest of him. He got one of my guns from Archie's desk, returned to this chair, opened the drawer where he had put the cushion, fired a shot into the cushion, dropped the gun in, and shut the drawer."

Wolfe sighed again. "Archie came dashing in, cast a glance at Mr. Root seated here, and went on to the front room. Mr. Root grasped the opportunity to do two things: return my gun to the drawer of Archie's

121

desk, and use a blade of his knife, I would guess the awl, to tear a gash in the corner of his ear. That of course improved the situation for him. But what improved it vastly more was the chance that came soon after, when Archie took him to the bathroom and left him there. He might have found another chance, but that was perfect. He entered the front room from the bathroom, put his own gun, handkerchief attached, in the vase, and returned to the bathroom, and later rejoined the others here."

"Jesus!" Purley Stebbins said incredulously. "That guy would jump off the Empire State Building to catch an airplane by the tail."

"No doubt," Wolfe agreed. "I have called him a fool; and yet it was by no means utterly preposterous if I had not noticed the absence of that cushion. Since this desk sits flush with the floor, no sign of the bullet fired into the bottom drawer would be visible unless the drawer was opened, and why should it be? It was unlikely that Archie would have occasion to find that one of my guns in his desk had been fired, and what if he did? Mr. Root knows how to handle a gun without leaving fingerprints, which is simple. Confound it, no. It was entirely feasible for him to await an opportunity to kill me, this evening, tonight, tomorrow morning, with all suspicion aimed at Miss Geer and Mr. Jensen—and disappear."

Cramer slowly nodded. "I'm not objecting. I'll buy it. But you must admit you've described quite a few things you can't prove."

"I don't have to. Neither do you. As I said before, Mr. Root will be put on trial for the murder of Mr. Jensen and Mr. Doyle, not for his antics here in my house. And I wish you would take him somewhere else. I've seen enough of him."

"I can't say I blame you," Cramer grinned, which was rare. He stood up. "Let's go, Mr. Root."

After letting them out and watching Cramer and Purley manipulating Hackett-Root down the steps to the sidewalk and into the police car, I shut the door without bothering about the bolt and returned to the office. Jane and Jensen were standing side by side in front of Wolfe's desk, just barely not holding hands, beaming down at him.

". . . more than neat," Jensen was saying. "It was absolutely brilliant."

"I still can't believe it," Jane declared. "It was wonderful."

"It was merely a job," Wolfe murmured, as if he knew what modesty was.

Nobody paid any attention to me. I sat down and yawned. Jensen seemed to be hesitating about something, then abruptly got it out.

"I owe you money. I came here Wednesday to engage you to investigate my father's murder. Later when the police got the crazy idea that I was involved in it, I was even more anxious to engage you, but still you wouldn't see me, and now of course I understand why. I may not be in debt to you legally, but I am morally, and it will be a great satisfaction to pay it. I haven't my checkbook with me, so I'll have to mail you one—say, five thousand dollars?"

Wolfe shook his head. "I accept pay only from clients, as arranged in advance. If you send me a check I'll have to return it. If you have to send one in order to sleep, send it to the National War Fund."

I managed to keep my face straight. As for Wolfe's renunciation, his income for the year had already reached a point where out of an additional five grand he would have been able to keep about one-fifth. As for Jensen's generosity, if it is okay for males at one age to climb trees and turn somersaults in the presence of females, why isn't it okay for them at another age to wave checkbooks? The way Jane was looking at him reminded me of the way a fifth-grade girl looked at me once, out in Ohio, when I chinned myself fourteen times.

So they settled it on a basis of reciprocal nobility, and the pair turned to go. Not caring to appear churlish, I went to open the front door for them. As they were passing through, Jane suddenly realized I was there and stopped and impulsively extended her hand.

"I take it back, Archie. You're not a rat. Shake on it. Is he, Emil?"

"He certainly is not," Emil baritoned heartily.

"Gee," I stammered with moist eyes, "this is the happiest day of my life. This will make a new rat of me," I closed the door.

Back in the office, Wolfe, in his own chair with only one bullet hole that could easily be repaired, and with three bottles of beer on a tray in front of him, was leaning back with his hands resting on the chair arms and his eyes open only to slits, the picture of a man at peace.

He murmured at me, "Archie. Don't forget to remind me in the morning to telephone Mr. Viscardi about that tarragon."

"Yes, sir." I sat down. "And if I may, sir, I would like to offer a suggestion."

"What?"

"Only a suggestion. Let's advertise for a man-eating tiger weighing around two hundred and sixty pounds capable of easy and normal movement. We could station him behind the big cabinet and when you enter he would leap on you from the rear."

It didn't faze him. He was enjoying the feel of his chair and I doubt if he heard me.

3 | Instead of Evidence

I

AMONG the kinds of men I have a prejudice against are the ones named Eugene. There's no use asking me why, because I admit it's a prejudice. It may be that when I was in kindergarten out in Ohio a man named Eugene stole candy from me, but if so I have forgotten all about it. For all practical purposes, it is merely one facet of my complex character that I do not like men named Eugene.

That and that alone accounted for my offish attitude when Mr. and Mrs. Eugene R. Poor called at Nero Wolfe's office that Tuesday afternoon in October, because I had never seen or heard of the guy before, and neither had Wolfe. The appointment had been made by phone that morning, so I was prejudiced before I ever got a look at him. The look hadn't swayed me much one way or the other. He wasn't too old to remember what his wife had given him on his fortieth birthday, but neither was he young enough to be still looking forward to it. Nothing about him stood out. His face was taken at random out of stock, with no alterations. Gray herringbone suits like his were that afternoon being bought in stores from San Diego to Bangor. Really his only distinction was that they had named him Eugene.

In spite of which I was regarding him with polite curiosity, for he had just told Nero Wolfe that he was going to be murdered by a man named Conroy Blaney.

I was sitting at my desk in the room Nero Wolfe used for an office in his home on West Thirty-fifth Street, and Wolfe was behind his desk, arranged in a chair that had been specially constructed to support up

125

to a quarter of a ton, which was not utterly beyond the limits of possibility. Eugene R. Poor was in the red leather chair a short distance beyond Wolfe's desk, with a little table smack against its right arm for the convenience of clients in writing checks. Mrs. Poor was on a spare between her husband and me.

I might mention that I was not aware of any prejudice against Mrs. Poor. For one thing, there was no reason to suppose that her name was Eugene. For another, there were several reasons to suppose that her fortieth birthday would not come before mine, though she was good and mature. She had by no means struck me dumb, but there are people who seem to improve a room just by being in it.

Naturally Wolfe was scowling. He shook his head, moving it a full half-inch right and left, which was for him a frenzy of negation.

"No, sir," he said emphatically. "I suppose two hundred men and women have sat in that chair, Mr. Poor, and tried to hire me to keep someone from killing them." His eyes twitched to me. "How many, Archie?"

I said, to oblige him, "Two hundred and nine."

"Have I taken the jobs?"

"No, sir. Never."

He wiggled a finger at Eugene. "For two million dollars a year you can make it fairly difficult for a man to kill you. That's about what it costs to protect a president or a king, and even so consider the record. Of course, if you give up all other activity it can be done more cheaply, say forty thousand a year. A cave in a mountainside, never emerging, with six guards you can trust and a staff to suit—"

Eugene was trying to get something in. He finally did. "I don't expect you to keep him from killing me. That's not what I came for."

"Then what the deuce did you come for?"

"To keep him from getting away with it." Eugene cleared his throat. "I was trying to tell you. I agree that you can't stop him, I don't see how anybody can. Sooner or later. He's a clever man." His voice took on bitterness. "Too damn clever for me and I wish I'd never met him. Sure, I know a man can kill a man if he once decides to, but Con Blaney is so damn clever

126

that it isn't a question whether he can kill me or not, the question is whether he can manage it so that he is in the clear. I'm afraid he can. I would bet he can. And I don't want him to."

His wife made a little noise and he stopped to look at her. Then he shook his head at her as if she had said something, took a cigar from his vest pocket, removed the band, inspected first one end and then the other to decide which was which, got a gadget from another vest pocket and snipped one of the ends, and lit up. He no sooner had it lit than it slipped out of his mouth, bounced on his thigh, and landed on the rug. He retrieved it and got his teeth sunk in it. So, I thought to myself, you're not so doggone calm about getting murdered as you were making out to be.

"So I came," he told Wolfe, "to give you the facts, to get the facts down, and to pay you five thousand dollars to see that he doesn't manage it that way." The cigar between his teeth interfered with his talking, and he removed it. "If he kills me I'll be dead. I want someone to know about it."

Wolfe's eyes had gone half shut. "But why pay me five thousand dollars in advance? Wouldn't someone know about it? Your wife, for instance?"

Eugene nodded. "I've thought about that. I've thought it all out. What if he kills her too? I have no idea how he'll try to work it, or when, and who is there besides my wife I can absolutely trust? I'm not taking any chances. Of course I thought of the police, but judging from my own experience, a couple of burglaries down at the shop, and you know, the experiences of a businessman, I'm not sure they'd even remember I'd been there if it happened in a year or maybe two years." He stuck his cigar in his mouth, puffed twice, and took it out again. "What's the matter, don't you want five thousand dollars?"

Wolfe said gruffly, "I wouldn't get five thousand. This is October. As my nineteen forty-five income now stands, I'll keep about ten per cent of any additional receipts after paying taxes. Out of five thousand, five hundred would be mine. If Mr. Blaney is as clever as you think he is, I wouldn't consider trying to uncover him on a murder for five hundred dollars." He stopped

127

and opened his eyes to glare at the wife. "May I ask, madam, what you are looking so pleased about?"

Wolfe couldn't stand to see a woman look pleased.

Mrs. Poor was regarding him with a little smile of obvious approval. "Because," she said, in a voice that was pleased too, and a nice voice, "I need help and I think you're going to help me. I don't approve of this. I didn't want my husband to come here."

"Indeed. Where did you want him to go, to the Atlantic Detective Agency?"

"Oh, no, if I had been in favor of his going to any detective at all, of course it would have been Nero Wolfe. But—may I explain?"

Wolfe glanced at the clock on the wall. Three-forty. In twenty minutes he would be leaving for the plant rooms on the roof, to monkey with the orchids. He said curtly, "I have eighteen minutes."

Eugene put in with a determined voice, "Then I'm going to use them—" But his wife smiled him out of it. She went on to Wolfe, "It won't take that long. My husband and Mr. Blaney have been business partners for ten years. They own the firm of Blaney and Poor, manufacturers of novelties—you know, they make things like matches that won't strike and chairs with rubber legs and bottled drinks that taste like soap—"

"Good God," Wolfe muttered in horror.

She ignored it. "It's the biggest firm in the business. Mr. Blaney gets the ideas and handles the production, he's a genius at it, and my husband handles the business part, sales and so on. But Mr. Blaney is really just about too conceited to live, and now that the business is a big success he thinks my husband isn't needed, and he wants him to get out and take twenty thousand dollars for his half. Of course it's worth a great deal more than that, at least ten times as much, and my husband won't do it. Mr. Blaney is very conceited, and also he will not let anything stand in his way. The argument has gone on and on, until now my husband is convinced that Mr. Blaney is capable of doing anything to get rid of him."

"Of killing him. And you don't agree."

"Oh, no. I do agree. I think Mr. Blaney would stop at nothing."

"Has he made threats?"

She shook her head. "He isn't that kind. He doesn't make threats, he just goes ahead."

"Then why didn't you want your husband to come to me?"

"Because he's simply too stubborn to live." She smiled at Eugene to take out any sting, and back at Wolfe. "There's a clause in the partnership agreement, they signed it when they started the business, that says if either one of them dies the other one owns the whole thing. That's another reason why my husband thinks Mr. Blaney will kill him, and I think so too. But what my husband wants is to make sure Mr. Blaney gets caught, that's how stubborn he is, and what *I* want is for my husband to stay alive."

"Now, Martha," Eugene put in, "I came here to—"

So her name was Martha. I had no prejudice against women named Martha.

She kept the floor. "It's like this," she appealed to Wolfe. "My husband thinks that Mr. Blaney is determined to kill him if he can't get what he wants any other way, and I think so too. You yourself think that if a man is determined to kill another man nothing can stop him. So isn't it perfectly obvious? My husband has over two hundred thousand dollars saved up outside the business, about half of it in war bonds. He can get another twenty thousand from Mr. Blaney for his half of the business—"

"It's worth twenty times that," Eugene said savagely, showing real emotion for the first time.

"Not to you if you're dead," she snapped back at him and went on to Wolfe. "With the income from that we could live more than comfortably—and happily. I hope my husband loves me—I *hope* he does—and I know I love him." She leaned forward in her chair. "That's why I came along today—I thought maybe you would help me persuade him. It isn't as if I wouldn't stand by my husband in a fight if there was any chance of his winning. But is there any sense in being so stubborn if you can't possibly win? Instead of winning you will probably die? Now does that make sense? I ask you, Mr. Wolfe, you are a wise and clever and able

129

man, what would you do if you were in my husband's position?"

Wolfe muttered, "You put that as a question?"

"Yes, I do."

"Well. Granting that you have described the situation correctly, I would kill Mr. Blaney."

She looked startled. "But that's silly." She frowned. "Of course you're joking, and it's no joke."

"I'd kill the bastard in a second," Eugene told Wolfe, "if I thought I could get away with it. I suppose you could, but I couldn't."

"And I'm afraid," Wolfe said politely, "you couldn't hire me for that." He glanced at the clock. "I would advise against your consulting even your wife. An undetected murder is strictly a one-man job. Her advice, sir, is sound. Are you going to take it?"

"No." Eugene sounded as stubborn as she said he was.

"Are you going to kill Mr. Blaney?"

"No."

"Do you still want to pay me five thousand dollars?"

"Yes, I do."

Mrs. Poor, who was rapidly becoming Martha to me, tried to horn in, but bigger and louder people than her had failed at that when orchid time was at hand. Wolfe ignored her and went on to him, "I advise you against that too, under the circumstances. Here are the circumstances—Archie, take your notebook. Make a receipt reading, 'Received from Eugene R. Poor five thousand dollars, in return for which I agree, in case he dies within one year, to give the police the information he has given to me today, and to take any further action that may seem to me advisable.' Sign my name and initial it as usual. Get all details from Mr. Poor." Wolfe pushed back his chair and got the levers of his muscles in position to hoist the bulk.

Eugene's eyes were moist with tears, but they came, not from emotion, but from smoke from his second cigar. In fact, throughout the interview his nervousness seemed to concentrate on his cigar. He had dropped it twice, and the smoke seemed determined to go down the wrong way and make him cough. But he was able to speak all right.

"That's no good," he objected. "You don't even say what kind of action. At least you ought to say—"

"I advised you against it under the circumstances." Wolfe was on his feet. "Those, sir, are the circumstances. That's all I'll undertake. Suit yourself." He started to move.

But Eugene had another round to fire. His hand went into a pocket and came out full of folded money. "I hadn't mentioned," he said, displaying the pretty objects, "that I brought it in cash. Speaking of income tax, if you're up to the ninety per cent bracket, getting it in cash would make it a lot more—"

Wolfe's look stopped him. "Pfui," Wolfe said. He hadn't had as good a chance to show off for a month. "I am not a common cheat, Mr. Poor. Not that I am a saint. Given adequate provocation, I might conceivably cheat a man—or woman or child, but a hundred and forty million of my fellow citizens. Bah."

We stared at his back as he left, as he knew we would, and in a moment we heard the sound of his elevator door opening.

I flipped to a fresh page in my notebook and turned to Eugene and Martha. "To refresh your memory," I said, "the name is Archie Goodwin, and I'm the one that does the work around here. I am also, Mr. Poor, an admirer of your wife."

He nearly dropped his cigar again. "You're what?"

"I admire your wife as an advice-giver. She has learned one of the most important rules, that far as life falls short of perfection it is more fun outside the grave than in it. With over two hundred thousand bucks—"

"I've had enough advice," he said as if he meant it. "My mind is made up."

"Okay." I got the notebook in position. "Give me everything you think we'll need. First, basic facts. Home and business addresses?"

It took close to an hour, so it was nearly five o'clock when they left. I found him irritating and therefore kept my prejudice intact. I wondered later what difference it would have made in my attitude if I had known that in a few hours he would be dead. Even if you take the line that he had it coming to him, which would be easy to justify, at least it would have made the situation more interesting. But during that hour, as far as I knew, they were just a couple of white-livers, scared stiff by a false alarm named Blaney, so it was merely another job.

I was still typing from my notes when at six o'clock, after the regulation two hours in the plant rooms, Wolfe came down to the office. He got fixed up in his chair, rang for Fritz to bring beer, and demanded, "Did you take that man's money?"

I grinned at him. Up to his old tricks. I had been a civilian again for only a week, and here he was already treating me like a hireling just as he had for years, acting as if I had never been a colonel, as in fact I hadn't, but anyway I had been a major.

I asked him, "What do you think? If I say I took it, you'll claim that your attitude as you left plainly indicated that he had insulted you and you wouldn't play. If I say I refused it, you'll claim I've done you out of a fee. Which do you prefer?"

He abandoned it. "Did you word the receipt properly?"

"No, sir. I worded it the way you told me to. The loot is in the safe and I'll deposit it tomorrow. I told him you'd prefer a check, but he said there it was, he had taken the trouble to get it, why not take it? He still thinks you'll forget to report it to your hundred and forty million fellow citizens. By the way, if Blaney does perform I'm going to marry the widow. Something unforeseen has happened. I have an ironclad rule that if the ankles are more than half as big around as the calves that settles it, I am absolutely not interested. But you saw her legs, and in spite of them I would rate her—"

"I did not see her legs. Do your typing. I like to hear you typing. If you are typing you can't talk."

To humor him I typed, which as it turned out was just as well, since that neat list of facts was going to be needed before bedtime. It was finished when Fritz entered at eight o'clock to announce dinner, the main item of which was a dish called by Wolfe and Fritz "Cassoulettes Castelnaudary," but by me boiled beans. I admit they were my favorite beans, which is saying

132

something. The only thing that restrained me at all was my advance knowledge of the pumpkin pie to come.

Back in the office, where the clock said nine-forty, I was just announcing my intention of catching a movie by the tail at the Rialto when the phone rang. It was Inspector Cramer, whose voice I hadn't heard for weeks, asking for Wolfe. Wolfe picked up his receiver, and I stuck to mine so as to get it firsthand.

"Wolfe? Cramer. I've got a paper here, taken from the pocket of a dead man, a receipt for five thousand dollars, signed by you, dated today. It says you have information to give the police if he dies. All right, he's dead. I don't ask you to come up here, because I know you wouldn't, and I'm too busy to go down there. What's the information?"

Wolfe grunted. "What killed him?"

"An explosion. Just give——"

"Did it kill his wife too?"

"Naw, she's okay, only overcome, you know. Just give——"

"I haven't got the information. Mr. Goodwin has it. Archie?"

I spoke up. "It would take quite a while, Inspector, and I've got it all typed. I can run up there——"

"All right, come ahead. The Poor apartment on Eighty-fourth Street. The number is——"

"I know the number. I know everything. Sit down and rest till I get there."

II

In the living room of an apartment on the sixth floor, on Eighty-fourth near Amsterdam Avenue, I stood and looked down at what was left of Eugene Poor. All I really recognized was the gray herringbone suit and the shirt and tie, on account of what the explosion had done to his face, and also on that account I didn't look much, for while I may not be a softy I see no point in prolonged staring at a face that has entirely stopped being a face.

I asked Sergeant Purley Stebbins, who was sticking

close by me, apparently to see that I didn't swipe Eugene's shoes, "You say a cigar did that to him?"

Purley nodded. "Yeah, so the wife says. He lit a cigar and it blew up."

"Huh. I don't believe it. Yes I guess I do too, if she says so. They make novelties. Now, that's a novelty."

I looked around. The room was full of what you would expect, assorted snoops, all doing the chores, from print collectors up to inspectors, or at least one inspector, namely Cramer himself, who sat at a table near a wall reading the script I had brought him. Most of them I knew, at least by sight, but there was one complete stranger. She was in a chair in a far corner, being questioned by a homicide dick named Rowcliff. Being trained to observe details even when under a strain, I had caught at a glance some of her outstanding characteristics, such as youth, shapeliness, and shallow depressions at the temples, which happen to appeal to me.

I aimed a thumb in her direction and asked Purley, "Bystander, wife's sister, or what?"

He shook his head. "God knows. She came to call just after we got here and we want to know what for."

"I hope Rowcliff doesn't abuse her. I would enjoy a murder where Rowcliff was the one that got it, and so would you."

I strolled over to the corner and stopped against them, and the girl and the dick looked up. "Excuse me," I told her, "when you get through here will you kindly call on Nero Wolfe at this address?" I handed her a card. The temples were even better close up. "Mr. Wolfe is going to solve this murder."

Rowcliff snarled. He always snarled. "Get away from here and stay away."

Actually he was helpless, because the inspector had sent for me and he knew it. I ignored him and told the temples, "If this person takes that card away from you, it's in the phone book, Nero Wolfe," left them and crossed over to Cramer at the table, dodging photographers and other scientists on the way.

Cramer didn't look up, so I asked the top of his head, "Where's Mrs. Poor?"

He growled, "Bedroom."

134

"I want to see her."

"The hell you do." He jiggled the sheets I had brought him to even the edges. "Sit down."

I sat down and said, "I want to see our client."

"So you've got a client?"

"Sure we have, didn't you see that receipt?"

He grunted. "Give her a chance. I am. Let her get herself together. Don't touch that!"

I was only moving a hand to point at a box of cigars there on the table, with the lid closed. I grinned at him. "The more the merrier. I mean fingerprints. But if that's the box the loaded one came from, you ought to satisfy my curiosity. He smoked two cigars this afternoon at the office."

He shot me a glance, then got out his penknife and opened the lid and lifted the paper flap. It was a box of twenty-five, and twenty-four of them were still there. Only one gone. I inspected at close range, sat back, and nodded. "They're the same. They not only look it, but the bands say Alta Vista. There would be two of those bands still in the ash tray down at the office if Fritz wasn't so neat." I squinted again at the array in the box. "They certainly look kosher. Do you suppose they're all loaded?"

"I don't know. The laboratory can answer that one." He closed the box with the tip of his knife. "Damn murders anyhow." He tapped the papers with his finger. "This is awful pat. The wife let out a hint or two, and I've sent for Blaney. I hope to God it's a wrap-up, and maybe it is. How did Poor seem this afternoon, scared, nervous, what?"

"Mostly stubborn. Mind made up."

"What about the wife?"

"Stubborn too. She wanted him to get out from under and go on breathing. She thought they could be as happy as larks on the income from a measly quarter of a million."

The next twenty minutes was a record—Inspector Cramer and me conversing without a single ugly remark. It lasted that long only because of various interruptions from his army. The last one, toward the end, was from Rowcliff walking up to the table to say:

"Do you want to talk to this young woman, Inspector?"

"How do I know? What about her?"

"Her name is Helen Vardis. She's an employee of Poor's firm, Blaney and Poor—been with them four years. At first she showed signs of hysteria and then calmed down. First she said she just happened to come here. Then she saw what that was worth and said she came to see Poor by appointment, at his request, on a confidential matter, and wants us to promise not to tell Blaney because she would lose her job."

"What confidential matter?"

"She won't say. That's what I've been working on."

"Work on it some more. She's got all night."

"Yes, sir. Goodwin gave her Nero Wolfe's card and told her to go to see him."

"Oh, he did. Go and work on her." Rowcliff left and Cramer glared at me. "You did?"

I looked hurt. "Certainly. Don't we have to do something to earn that five grand?"

"I don't know why, since you've already got it. How would you like to go somewhere else? Next thing you'll be liberating this box of cigars or maybe the corpse, and I can't spare a squad to watch—now what?"

There was a commotion at the outer door, and it came on through the foyer into the living room in the shape of a municipal criminologist gripping the arm of a wild-eyed young man who apparently didn't want to be gripped. They were both talking, or at least making noises. It was hard to tell whether they were being propelled by the young man pulling or the cop pushing.

Cramer boomed, "Doyle! What the hell? Who is that?"

The young man goggled around, declaiming, "I have a right—oh!"

It might have been supposed that what had stopped him was the sight of Poor's body, especially the face, but his eyes weren't aimed that way. They were focused toward the far corner where Rowcliff was working on the girl. She was focusing back at him, rising slowly to her feet, her lips moving without opening. They stared at each other long enough to count ten, with everyone else in the room knocking off to watch the charade.

The young man said, as if he was conveying information, "There you are."

She said, as if she didn't need any information from snakes or rats, "You didn't lose any time, did you? Now you think you can have her, don't you?"

He held the stare, showing no reaction except clamping his jaw, and their audience sat tight. In a moment he seemed to realize it was rather a public performance, and his head started to pivot, doing a slow circle, taking in the surroundings. It was a good thorough job of looking, without any waver or pause, so far as I could see, even when it hit the most sensational item, namely, the corpse. During the process his eyes lost their wild look entirely, and when he spoke his voice was cool and controlled. It was evident that his mental operations were enough in order for him to pick the most intelligent face in the bunch, since it was to me he put the question.

"Are you in charge here?"

I replied, "No. This one. Inspector Cramer."

He strode across and looked Cramer in the eye and made a speech. "My name is Joe Groll. I work for Blaney and Poor, factory foreman. I followed that girl, Helen Vardis, when she left home tonight, because I wanted to know where she was going, and came here. The police cars and cops going in and out made me want to ask questions, and finally I got the answer that a man named Poor had been murdered, so I wanted to find out. Where is Blaney? Conroy Blaney, the partner—"

"I know," Cramer said, looking disgusted. Naturally he was disgusted, since what he had hoped would be a wrap-up was spilling out in various directions. "We've sent for Blaney. Why were you following—"

"That isn't true!"

More diversions. Helen Vardis had busted out of her corner to join the table group, close enough to Joe Groll to touch him, but they weren't touching. Instead of resuming their staring match, they were both intent on Cramer.

137

Looking even more disgusted, Cramer asked her, "What isn't true?"

"That he was following me!" Helen was mad clear to her temples and pretty as a picture. "Why should he follow me? He came here to—"

She bit it off sharp.

"Yeah," Cramer said encouragingly. "To what?"

"I don't know! But I do know who killed Mr. Poor! It was Martha Davis!"

"That helps. Who is Martha Davis?"

Joe Groll said, giving information again, "She means Mrs. Poor. That was her name when she worked in the factory, before she got married. She means Mrs. Poor killed her husband. That's on account of jealousy. She's crazy."

A quiet but energetic voice came from a new direction. "She certainly is."

It was Martha, who emerged from a door at the far end and approached the table. She was pale and didn't seem any too sure of her leg action, but she made her objective all right. She spoke to the girl, with no sign of violent emotion that I could detect, not even resentment.

"Helen, you ought to be ashamed of yourself. I think you will be when you have calmed down and thought things over. You have no right or reason to talk like that. You accuse me of killing my husband? Why?"

Very likely Helen would have proceeded to tell her why. She was obviously in the mood for it, and it was one of those set-ups when people blurt things that you couldn't get out of them an hour later with a stomach pump. Any sap knows that, and Cramer was not quite a sap, so when at that moment a cop entered from the foyer escorting a stranger Cramer motioned with his hand for them to back out. But the stranger was not a backer-out. He came on straight to the table and, since the arrangement showed plainly that Cramer was it, addressed the inspector.

"I'm Conroy Blaney. Where's Gene Poor?"

Not that he was aggressive or in any way overwhelming. His voice was a tenor squeak and it fitted his looks. I could have picked him up and set him down again without grunting; he had an undersized nose and

138

not much chin, and he was going bald. But in spite of all those handicaps his sudden appearance had a remarkable effect. Martha Poor simply turned and left the room. The expressions on the faces of Helen Vardis and Joe Groll changed completely; they went deadpan in one second flat. I saw at once that there would be no more blurting, and so did Cramer.

As for Blaney, he looked around, saw the body of his partner on the floor, stepped toward it and gazed down at it, and squeaked, "Good heavens. Good Heavens! Who did it?"

III

Next morning at eleven o'clock, when Wolfe came down to the office after his two-hour morning session up in the plant rooms, I made my report. He took it, as usual, leaning back in his chair with his eyes closed, with no visible sign of consciousness. The final chapter was the details given me by Martha Poor, with whom I had managed to have a talk around midnight by pressing Cramer on the client angle and wearing him down. I gave it to Wolfe.

"They came here yesterday in their own car. When they left here, a little before five, they drove to Madison Square Garden and got a program of the afternoon rodeo performance, the reason for that being he had needed to explain his absence from the office and not wanting Blaney to know that he was coming to see you, he had said he was going to the rodeo and wanted to be able to answer questions if he was asked about it. Then they drove up to Westchester. Conroy Blaney has a place up there, a shack in the hills where he lives and spends his evenings and week ends thinking up novelties, and they had a date to see him there and discuss things. Mrs. Poor had persuaded Poor to go, thinking they might reach an agreement, but Poor hadn't wanted to, and on the way up he balked, so they stopped at a place near Scarsdale, Monty's Tavern, to debate. Poor won the debate. He wouldn't go. She left him at the tavern and went on to Blaney's place alone. The date was for six-fifteen and she got there right on the dot. Are you awake?"

He grunted.

I went on, "Blaney wasn't there. He lives alone, and the doors were locked. She waited around and got cold. At ten minutes to seven she beat it back to the tavern. She and Poor ate dinner there, then drove back to town, put the car in the garage, and went home. Poor had had no cigar after dinner because they hadn't had his brand at the tavern and he wouldn't smoke anything else. He has been smoking Alta Vistas for years, ten to fifteen a day. So he hung up his hat and opened a fresh box. She didn't see him do it because she was in the bathroom. She heard the sound of the explosion, not very loud, and ran out and there he was. She phoned downstairs, and the elevator man and hall man came and phoned for a doctor and the police. Still awake?"

He grunted again.

"Okay. That's it. When I returned to the living room everyone had left, including Poor's leftovers. Some friend had come to spend the night, and of course there was a cop out in the hall. When I got home you were in bed, snoring."

He had long ago quit bothering to deny that he snored. Now he didn't bother about anything, but just sat there. I resumed with the plant records. Noon came and went, and still he was making no visible effort to earn five thousand dollars, or even five hundred.

Finally he heaved a sigh, almost opened his eyes, and told me, "You say the face was unrecognizable."

"Yes, sir. As I described it."

"From something concealed in a cigar. Next to incredible. Phone Mr. Cramer. Tell him it is important that the identity of the corpse be established beyond question. Also that I want to see a photograph of Mr. Poor while still intact."

I goggled at him. "For God's sake, what do you think? That she doesn't know her own husband? She came home with him. Now really. The old insurance gag? Your mind's in a rut. I will not phone Mr. Cramer merely to put myself on the receiving end of a horse laugh."

"Be quiet. Let me alone. Phone Mr. Cramer."

And that was all. Apparently he thought he had earned his fee. No instructions to go get Helen Vardis or Joe Groll or Blaney or even Martha Poor. When I phoned Cramer he didn't laugh, but that was only because he had stopped laughing at Nero Wolfe some time back. I gritted my teeth and went on with the plant records.

At lunch he discussed Yugoslav politics. That was all right, because he never talked business at the table, but when, back in the office, he went through the elaborate operations of getting himself settled with the atlas, I decided to apply spurs and sink them deep.

I arose and confronted him and announced, "I resign."

He muttered testily without looking up, "Nonsense. Do your work."

"No, sir. I'm going upstairs to pack. If you're too lazy to wiggle a finger, very well, that's not news. But you could at least send me to the public library to look up the genealogy—"

"Confound it!" He glared at me. "I engaged to give that information to the police and have done so. Also to take any further action that might seem to me advisable. I have done that."

"Do you mean you're through with the case?"

"Certainly not. I haven't even started, because there's nothing to start on. Mr. Cramer may do the job himself, or he may not. I hope he does. If you don't want to work, go to a movie."

I went upstairs to my room and tried to read a book, knowing it wouldn't work because I can never settle down when a murder case is on. So I returned to the office and rattled papers, but even that didn't faze him. At four o'clock, when he went up to the plant rooms, I went to the corner and got afternoon papers, but there was nothing in them but the usual crap. When he came down again at six it was more of the same, and I went out for a walk to keep from throwing a chair at him, and stayed until dinnertime. After dinner I went to a movie, and when I got home a little after eleven and found him sitting drinking beer and reading a magazine, I went upstairs to bed without saying good night.

141

Next morning, Thursday, there wasn't a peep out of him before nine o'clock, the time he went up to the damn orchids. When Fritz came down with the breakfast tray from Wolfe's room, with nothing left on the dishes to wash off, I asked him, "How's the pet mammoth?"

"Very difficult," Fritz said in a satisfied tone. "*Refrogné*. Always in the morning. Healthy."

I read the papers and had more coffee.

When Wolfe came down to the office at eleven I greeted him with a friendly suggestion. "Look," I said, "you're an expert on murder. But this Poor murder bores you because you've already collected your fee. So how about this?" I spread the morning Gazette on his desk and indicated. "Absolutely Grade A. Man's naked body found in an old orchard off a lonely lane four miles from White Plains, head crushed to a pancake, apparently by a car running square over him. It offers many advantages to a great detective like you. It might be Hitler, since his body has never been found. It is in a convenient neighborhood, easily reached by trains, bus, or auto, electric lights and city gas. The man has been dead at least thirty-six hours, counting from now, so it has the antique quality you like, with the clues all—"

In another minute I would have had him sputtering with fury, but the doorbell rang. "Study it," I told him, and went to the hall and the front and, following routine, fingered the curtain edge aside for a look through the glass panel.

After one brief glance I went back to the office and told Wolfe casually, "It's only Cramer. To hell with him. Since he's working on the Poor case and you're not interested—"

"Archie. Confound you. Bring him in."

The bell was ringing again, and that irritates me, so I went and got him. He was wearing his raincoat and his determined look. I relieved him of the former in the hall and let him take the latter on into the office. When I joined them Cramer was lowering himself into the red leather chair and telling Wolfe, "I dropped in on my way uptown because I thought it was only fair since you gave me that information. I think I'm going to arrest your client on a charge of murder."

I sat down and felt at home.

IV

Wolfe grunted. He leaned back in his chair, got his fingertips touching in the locality of his belly button, and said offensively, "Nonsense. You can't arrest my client on any charge whatever. My client is dead. By the way, is he? Has the corpse been properly identified?"

Cramer nodded. "Certainly. With a face like that it's routine. Barber, dentist, and doctor—they're the experts. Why, what did you think it was, an insurance fake?"

"I didn't think. Then you can't arrest my client."

"Goodwin says Mrs. Poor is your client."

"Mr. Goodwin is impulsive. You read that receipt. So you're going to charge Mrs. Poor?"

"I think I am."

"Indeed."

Cramer scowled at him. "Don't indeed me. Goddam it, didn't I take the trouble to stop and tell you about it?"

"Go ahead and tell me."

"Very well." Cramer screwed up his lips, deciding where to start. "First I'd appreciate an answer to a question. What is this identity angle anyhow? There's not the slightest doubt it was Poor. Not only the corpse itself, other things, like the elevator man that took them up when they came home, and the people up at the tavern where they ate dinner. He was known there. And what did you want a photograph for?"

"Did you bring one?"

"No. Apparently there aren't any. I wasn't interested after the dentist and barber verified the corpse, but I understand the papers had to settle for sketches drawn from descriptions. One reason I came here, what's your idea doubting the identity of the corpse?"

Wolfe shook his head. "Evidently silly, since you're ready to take Mrs. Poor. You were telling me . . ."

"Yeah. Of course Goodwin told you about the box of cigars."

"Something."

"Well, that was it all right. Poor smoked about a box every two days, boxes of twenty-five. He bought them, ten boxes at a time, from a place on Varick Street near his office and factory. There were four unopened boxes in his apartment and they're okay. The one he started on when he got home Tuesday night—the twenty-four left in it are all loaded. Any one of them would have killed him two seconds after he lit it."

Wolfe muttered, "That's hard to believe—inside a cigar—"

"Right. I thought so too. The firm of Blaney and Poor has been making trick cigars for years, but they're harmless, all they do is phut and make you jump. What's in these twenty-four is anything but harmless—a special kind of instantaneous fuse the size of an ordinary thread, and a very special explosive capsule that was invented during the war and is still on the secret list. Even this is confidential, it's made by the Beck Products Corporation, and their men and the FBI are raising hell trying to find out how this murderer got hold of them. That's not for publication."

"I'm not a publisher."

"Okay." Cramer got a cigar from his pocket, gazed at it with an attention that was not his habit, bit off an end, and lit it. Wolfe and I watched the operation, which we had both seen Cramer perform at least two hundred times, as if there was something very interesting about it.

"Of course," Wolfe remarked, "the Alta Vista people deny all knowledge."

"Sure. We let them analyze five of the twenty-four, after removing the fuses and capsules, and they say the fillers are theirs but the wrappers are not. They say whoever sliced them open and inserted the things and rewrapped them was an expert, and anyhow, anybody could see that." Cramer sank his teeth deeper in his cigar. "Now then. There are six people connected with Blaney and Poor who are good at making trick cigars. Four of them are mixed up in this. Helen Vardis is one of their most highly skilled workers. Joe Groll is the foreman and can do anything. Blaney is the best of all, he shows them how. And Mrs. Poor worked there for four years when she was Martha Davis, up to two years ago when she married Poor."

Wolfe shuddered. "Six people good at making trick cigars. Couldn't the murder have been a joint enterprise? Couldn't you convict all of them?"

"I don't appreciate jokes about murder," Cramer said morosely. "I wish I could. It's a defect of character. As for getting the loaded cigars into Poor's apartment, that also is wide open. He always had them delivered to his office, and the package would lie around there, sometimes as long as two or three days, until he took it home. So anybody might have substituted the loaded box. But now about Mrs. Poor. How do you like this? Naturally we gave the cigars and the box everything we had. It was a very neat job. But underneath the cigars we found two human hairs, one five inches long and one six and a half inches. We have compared them with hairs taken from various heads. Those two came from the head of Mrs. Poor. Unquestionably. So I think I'll charge her."

Wolfe grunted and shut his eyes.

I asked, perfectly friendly, "Hairs don't have arches and loops and whorls, do they, Inspector?"

"Nuts." He glared at me. "Where's your laboratory?"

Wolfe's eyes half opened. "I wouldn't do it if I were you, Mr. Cramer."

"Oh." He glared at Wolfe. "You wouldn't."

"No, sir. Let me put it this way." Wolfe maneuvered himself into position for an uplift and got to his feet. "You have her on trial. The hairs have been placed in evidence. I am the defense attorney. I am speaking to the jury."

Wolfe fixed his eyes on me. "Ladies and gentlemen, I respect your intelligence. The operation of turning those cigars into deadly bombs has been described to you as one requiring the highest degree of skill and the minutest attention. Deft fingers and perfect eyesight were essential. Since the slightest irregularity about the appearance of that box of cigars might have attracted the attention of a veteran smoker, you can imagine the anxious scrutiny with which each cigar was inspected as it was arranged in the box. And you can realize how incredible it is that such a person, so intently engaged on anything and everything the eye could see, could possibly have been guilty of such atrocious carelessness as to leave two of the hairs of her head in that box with those cigars. Ladies and gentlemen, I appeal to your intelligence! I put it to you that those hairs, far from being evidence that Martha Poor killed her husband, are instead evidence that Martha Poor did not kill her husband!"

Wolfe sat down and muttered, "Then they acquit her, and whom do you charge next?"

Cramer growled, "So she is your client after all."

"No, sir, she is not. It was Mr. Poor who paid me. You said you came here because you wanted to be fair. Pfui. You came here because you had misgivings. You had them because you are not a ninny. A jury would want to know, anyone concerned would want to know, if those hairs did not get in the box through Mrs. Poor's carelessness, how did they get there? Who has had access to Mrs. Poor's head or hairbrush? Manifestly that is a forlorn hope. The best chance, I would say, is the explosive capsules. Discover the tiniest link between anyone of the Beck Products Corporation and one of your suspects, and you have it, if not your case, at least your certainty. On that I couldn't help, since I am no longer connected with the War Department. You can't convict anybody at all, let alone Mrs. Poor, without an explanation of how he got the capsules. By the way, what about motive? Mrs. Poor was tired of smelling the smoke from her husband's cigars, perhaps?"

"No. Poor was a tightwad and she wanted money. She gets the whole works plus a hundred thousand insurance. Or according to that girl, Helen Vardis, she wanted Joe Groll and now they'll get married."

"Proof?"

"Oh, talk." Cramer looked frustrated. "It goes away back to when Mrs. Poor was working there. I'll tell you this, whether she's your client or not. Naturally we've been having conversation with everybody at Blaney and Poor's, both office and factory. The females all go thumbs down on her, the idea being that she's a maneater. The males, just the opposite. According to them, she's as pure as soap. Old-fashioned stick candy. If you ask me, another good reason for charging her."

"Specifications? By the females?"

"No. None. But it's unanimous."

"It would be." Wolfe waved it away with a finger. "She married the proprietor." He frowned. "Another thing, Mr. Cramer, about a jury. As you know, I am strongly disinclined to leave this house for any purpose whatever. I detest the idea of leaving it to go to a courtroom and sit for hours on those wooden abominations they think are seats, and the thing they provide for witnesses is even worse. I would strain a point to avoid that experience; but if it can't be avoided Mr. Goodwin and I shall have to testify that Mr. Poor sat in that chair and told us of his conviction that Mr. Blaney was going to kill him. You know juries; you know how that would affect them. Suppose, again, that I am the defense attorney and—"

God help us, I thought, he's going to address the jury again. But I got a break in the form of an excuse to skip it when the doorbell rang. Winking at Cramer as I passed him on my way to the hall, I proceeded to the front door and took a peek. What I saw seemed to call for finesse, so I opened the door just enough to slip through out to the stoop, shut the door behind me, and said, "Hello, let's have a little conference."

Conroy Blaney squeaked at me. "What's the idea?"

I grinned at him amiably. "A policeman named Cramer is in Mr. Wolfe's office having a talk, and I thought maybe you had had enough of him for a while. Unless you're tailing him?"

"Inspector Cramer?"

I don't know how he did it. Basically and visibly he was a chinless bald-headed runt, and his voice sounded like a hinge that needed oil, but there was something in the way he said Inspector Cramer that gave the double impression that (a) there was a rumor going around that Cramer did actually exist, and (b) that if he did exist Conroy Blaney could make him stop existing by lifting a finger if he wanted to. I regarded him with admiration.

"Yes," I said. "Are you tailing him?"

"Good heavens, no. I want to see Nero Wolfe."

"Okay, then follow me, and after we are inside, don't talk. Get it?"

"I want to see Nero Wolfe immediately."

"Will you follow instructions or won't you? Do you also want to see Cramer?"

"Very well, open the door."

As I inserted my key I was telling myself, murderer or not, I am going to be wishing this specimen was big enough to plug in the jaw before this is finished. He did, however, obey orders. I conducted him into the front room, the door connecting it with the office being closed, left him there on a chair and went back by way of the hall.

"It can't wait," I told Wolfe. "The man from Plehn's with the Dendrobiums."

But a minute later Cramer was standing up to go. Knowing how suspicious he was, as well as how many good reasons he had had for being suspicious on those premises, and also knowing how cops in general love to open doors that don't belong to them just to stick a head in, I escorted him to the front and let him out, then returned to the office and told Wolfe who the company was.

Wolfe frowned. "What does he want?"

"I think he wants to confess. I warn you, his squeak will get on your nerves."

"Bring him in."

V

I expected to enjoy it and I did, only it didn't last long. Blaney started off by rejecting the red leather chair and choosing one of the spares, which irritated both of us, since we like our routine.

Perched on it, he began, "I was thinking on my way here, fate has thrown us together, Wolfe. You dominate your field and I dominate mine. We were bound to meet."

It caught Wolfe so completely off balance that he only muttered sarcastically, "Your field."

"That's right." In profile, from where I sat, Blaney looked like a gopher. "I am supreme. I imagine you and I are alike in more ways than one. Now I like to see things done in an orderly manner. So do you, don't you?"

Wolfe was speechless. But Blaney, obviously not giving a damn how he was, went on, "So first I'll give you my four reasons for coming here and then we can take them up one at a time. One: I want a copy of the report you gave the police of what Gene Poor and Martha, his wife, told you about me. Two: discussion of whether your giving that report to the police was publication of a libel, and whether your withdrawal of it will satisfy me. Three: description of several methods by which I could kill a man without the slightest chance of detection. Four: a proposal to make an orchid, guaranteed exclusive to you, an imitation orchid plant in a pot, growing and blooming, that would talk! When the pot was lifted it would say distinctly, 'Orchids to you!' or anything of similar length."

"Good heavens," Wolfe muttered incredulously.

Blaney nodded with satisfaction. "I knew we would have many things in common. That's my favorite expression, I use it all the time—good heavens. But you probably want to know where I stand, I would if I were you. I did not come here because of any fear on my own account. There is not the remotest chance of my safety being endangered. But Tuesday evening up at Gene's apartment I heard a man saying to another man—I presume they were detectives—something about Mrs. Poor being Nero Wolfe's client and in that case Mrs. Poor was as good as out of it, and Nero Wolfe had decided on Blaney and if so Blaney might as well get his leg shaved for the electrode. I knew that might be just talk, but I really think it would be a shame for you to make yourself ridiculous, and I don't think you want to. I'm willing to take this trouble. You're not a man to reach a conclusion without reasons. That wouldn't be scientific, and you and I are both scientists. Tell me your reasons, one by one, and I'll prove they're no good. Go ahead."

"Archie." Wolfe looked at me. "Get him out of here."

There wasn't the slightest indication from Blaney

149

that anyone had said anything except him, and I was too fascinated to move.

Blaney went on, "The truth is, you have no reasons. The fact that Gene was afraid I would kill him proves nothing. He was a born coward. I did describe to him some of the methods by which I could kill a man without detection, but that was merely to impress upon him the fact that he continued to own half of the business by my sufferance and therefore my offer of twenty thousand dollars for his half was an act of generosity. I wouldn't condescend to kill a man. No man is worth that much to me, or that little."

As he went on his squeak showed a tendency to hoarsen.

"So you have no reasons. I suspected you didn't, but if you did I wanted to answer them. We can go back to my one, two, and three later, but right now about this talking orchid. When I get hold of a creative idea I can't concentrate on anything else. You will have to give me three or four orchid plants to work from, and they ought to be your favorite plants. And here's the stroke of genius, I was saving this, the voice that does the talking will be—your voice! Whoever you send it to, preferably a lady, she will lift the pot, suspecting nothing, and your own voice, the voice of Nero Wolfe, will say to her, *Orchids to you!* Probably she'll drop the pot. But—"

He had performed a miracle. I saw it with my own eyes. Nero Wolfe fleeing in haste from his own office. He had chased many a fellow being from that room, but that was the first time he had ever himself been chased. It became evident that he wasn't even going to risk staying on that floor when the sound was heard of the door of his elevator banging open and shut.

I told Blaney, "Overlook it. He's eccentric."

Blaney said, "So am I."

I nodded. "Geniuses are."

Blaney was frowning. "Does he really think I killed Gene Poor?"

"Yeah. He does now."

"Why now?"

I waved it away. "Forget it. I'm eccentric too."

Blaney was still frowning. "There's another possibil-

150

ity. The idea of the orchid having his voice doesn't appeal to him. Then how about its having your voice? You have a good baritone voice. I would let you have it at cost, and you could give it to him for Christmas. Let's see how it would sound. Say it in a medium tone, *Orchids to you*—"

The house phone buzzed, and I swung my chair around and took it. It was Wolfe, on his room extension.

"Archie. Is that man gone?"

"No, sir. He wants me—"

"Get him out of there at once. Phone Saul and tell him to come here as soon as possible."

"Yes, sir."

The line went dead. So he had actually been stirred up enough to blow some dough on the case. Saul Panzer, being merely the best all-around investigator west of Nantucket, not counting me, came to twenty bucks a day plus expenses.

To get Blaney out I nearly had to carry him.

VI

As luck would have it, Saul Panzer was not to be had at the moment. Since he was free-lancing, you never knew. I finally got it that he was out on Long Island on a job for Atlantic and left word for him to call. He did so around three and said he would be able to get to the office soon after six o'clock.

It became obvious that to Wolfe, who had been stirred up, money was no object, since he blew another dollar and eighty cents on a phone call to Washington. I got through without any trouble to General Carpenter, head of G-2, under whom I had been a major and for whom Wolfe had helped to solve certain problems connected with the war. The favor he asked of Carpenter, and of course got, was a telegram that would open doors at the premises of the Beck Products Corporation.

Not satisfied with that, he opened another valve. At ten minutes to four he said to me, "Archie. Find out

151

whether it seems advisable for me to talk with that man Joe Groll."

"Yes, sir. Tea leaves? Or there's a palmist over on Seventh—"

"See him and find out. Why did he ask where Blaney was up there Tuesday evening? Anything else."

"As, for instance, when does he marry Mrs. Poor and did she ever eat him?"

"Anything."

So after he went up to the plant rooms I phoned the office of Blaney and Poor and got Joe Groll. No persuasion was required. His tone implied that he would be glad to talk with anybody, any time, anywhere, after business hours. He would be free at five-thirty. I told him I'd be waiting for him at the corner of Varick and Adams in a brown Wethersill sedan.

He was twenty minutes late. "Sorry to keep you waiting," he apologized as he climbed in front beside me. "I only quit being a GI hero two months ago, and they gave me my old job back, and it keeps me busy catching up."

His glance at me was a question, but I postponed answering it, because my eye being used to taking in things, I had noticed something on the sidewalk in the twilight. Sure enough, as I let the clutch in and we slid away from the sidewalk, somebody's desire to find a taxi got practically frantic. To oblige, I took my time. When I saw in the mirror that a taxi had actually been snagged, I fed gas and went ahead. Then I answered the question his glance had asked.

"I don't sport a ruptured duck because I didn't get over to kill any Germans. They gave me a majority so I could run errands for Nero Wolfe while he was winning the war. There's a bar and grill on Nineteenth Street that has good Scotch. All right?"

He didn't object, so I kept my course, crowding no lights so as not to complicate matters for the taxi behind. Its driver was no bargain, because when I pulled up in front of Pete's Bar & Grill, instead of going on by the sap swerved toward the curb not more than thirty yards back.

In addition to good Scotch, Pete's had booths partitioned to the ceiling, which furnished privacy. Seated in

152

one of them, I was surprised to realize that you could make out a case for calling Joe Groll handsome. They had overdone it a little on the ears, but on the whole he was at least up to grade if not fancy. After we got our drinks I remarked casually, "As I told you on the phone, I want to discuss this murder. You may have heard of Nero Wolfe. Poor and his wife came to see him Tuesday afternoon, to tell him Blaney was going to dissolve the partnership by killing Poor."

He nodded. "Yes, I know."

"Oh. The cops told you?"

"No, Martha told me yesterday. Mrs. Poor. She asked me to come up and help about things—the funeral." He made a gesture. "Gosh, one lousy civilian funeral makes more fuss than a thousand dead men over there did."

I nodded. "Sure, the retail business always has more headaches than the wholesale." I sipped my highball. "I don't go for this theory that it was Helen Vardis that killed Poor. Do you?"

"What?" He stared. "What are you talking about? What theory?" His fingers had tightened around his glass.

"Why, this idea that Helen Vardis would do anything for Blaney, God knows why, and she made the cigars for him, and she went there Tuesday night—"

"Well, for Christ's sake." He said that calmly, and then suddenly his voice went up high. "Who thought that one up. Was it that cop Rowcliff? That buzzard? Was it Nero Wolfe? Was it you?"

He sounded next door to hysterical. I sure had pushed the wrong button, or maybe the right one, but I didn't want him sore at me. "It wasn't me," I assured him. "Don't get excited."

He laughed. It sounded bitter but not hysterical. "That's right," he said, "I must remember that, not to get excited. Everybody is very thoughtful. They put you in uniform and teach you what every young man ought to know, and take you across the ocean into the middle of hell, bombs, bullets, shells, flame-throwers, your friends die right against you and bleed down your neck, and after two years of that they bring you home and turn you loose and tell you now remember don't get excited."

He drank his highball, clear to the bottom, and put his glass down. "I'm all right," he said calmly. "So I am loose again and come back to my job. Don't get excited. Here's what I find. A girl I had been sort of counting on, named Martha Davis, has married the boss and no one told me. It wasn't her fault, she never promised me anything, not even to write to me, but I had been looking forward to seeing her. Oh, I saw her, because she was in trouble and asked me to help. She thought her husband was going to get killed, and knowing Blaney as I did I saw no reason to doubt it. I met her places a few times because she wanted to talk it over with me, and she wanted me to watch Blaney. Why am I spilling all this to you? You weren't in the Army."

"I was in the Army," I said, "but I admit nobody bled down my neck. I did what I was told."

"So did I, brother. Didn't we all. Anyhow, I wasn't heartbroken, because she seemed a little older than I had remembered her, and besides there was another girl who had been nothing but a kid in the factory but she had grown up. I'm not telling you anything the cops don't know. God, the cops are something! That's Helen Vardis. You saw her the other night."

"Yeah, she seemed upset."

"Upset?" He laughed a one-second laugh. "She sure was upset. I fell for her like a Sherman tank roaring down a cliff. I certainly hit bottom—All right, I guess I will. Thanks."

That was for the second drink, arriving. He picked it up and swallowed half.

"It is good Scotch. She seemed to reciprocate. I guess I was a little leery of all civilians, even her, but she seemed to reciprocate. I can't understand what that guy Poor had that attracted girls, and at his age, too. That I will never understand. First Martha, and then her. I saw her with him in a restaurant. Then I saw them together in his car. Then I followed her from the office and watched her meet him on Fourteenth Street, and they took a taxi and I lost them. Naturally I sprung it on her, and she the same as told me to go to hell. She refused to explain."

He finished the drink. "So they say don't get excited. The cops told me yesterday, and again today, don't get excited. Which one is it that thinks Helen Vardis was helping Blaney? Is it you?"

I shook my head. "I am not a cop. It's just something I heard and I wondered what you thought of it. In a murder case you're apt to hear anything."

"Why do you listen?"

"Why not? I'm listening to you."

He laughed, somewhat better. "You're a hell of a guy to work on a murder. You don't try to hammer me and you don't try to uncle. Do you want to come along and help me do something?"

"I might if you'd describe it. I promised my mother I would always be helpful to people."

"Wait a minute. I want to make a phone call."

He slid along the seat and left the booth. I sipped my highball and lit a cigarette, wondering whether the feel of blood going down his neck had really loosened a screw in him or if he was just temporarily rattled. In less than five minutes he was back, sliding along the seat again, and announcing, "Blaney's up at his place in Westchester. I phoned to ask him about a job we're doing, but really to find out if he was up there."

"Good. Now we know. Is that where we're going?"

"No." He gazed at his glass. "I thought I drank that—oh. You had it filled again. Thanks." He took some. "Anyway, that idea about Helen is silly because it was obviously either Martha or Blaney, if the cops have any brains at all. Martha says she went to Blaney's place in Westchester at six-fifteen Tuesday to keep a date she and Poor had with him, and there was no one there and she waited around until ten minutes to seven. Blaney says he was there all the time, from a quarter to six on, all evening, until he got the phone call from the police that Poor had been killed. So one of them is lying, and the one that's lying is obviously the one that killed Poor. So it's Blaney."

"Why, because Martha wouldn't lie?"

He frowned at me. "Now don't smart up. What the hell would she kill him for? She only got him two years

155

ago and he had everything he ever had. Anyway, it was Blaney, and I am fed up with all the gear-grinding, and he is now through with me and I'll be out of a job, so to hell with him. I'm going to see what I can find. On account of the trick cigars the cops wanted to go through the office and factory, and Blaney told them sure, go ahead, go as far as you like, but he didn't tell them about the abditories and they didn't find them."

"How do you spell it?"

He spelled it. "Abditory. Place to hide things. Blaney says it's a scientific term. The office is full of them. I haven't had a chance before now since Tuesday night, but with him up in Westchester I'm going to take a look. With a nut like Blaney you never can tell. Want to come along?"

"Have you got keys?"

"Keys? I'm the foreman."

"Okay, finish your drink."

He did so, and I got the bill and paid it, and we got our hats and coats and emerged. Meanwhile I was considering a complication and deciding how to handle it. Of course with the sedan I could have lost a dozen taxis if I had wanted to, but it would take time and gas and wear on the tires, and anyhow, the way it was shaping up, it seemed uncalled for. So when we were on the sidewalk alongside the sedan I asked him to wait a minute, marched back to where the taxi was still parked, jerked the door open and stuck my head in, and said, "There's no sense in this, Helen. Look at that meter! Come on and ride with us."

Even in the dim light she recognized me at the first glance, which I took as a compliment. After gasping, she left her mouth hanging open, but in spite of that handicap no one with an eye for essentials would have had any fault to find with the outlook, or perhaps I should say the inlook.

She re-established control of her jaw muscles enough to say briefly, "Get out!"

"Lookit, mister—" the taxi driver began like a menace.

"Everybody relax," I said pleasantly. "I can't get out because I'm not in, I'm only looking in." I told the temples, "This is absolutely childish. You don't know the first principle of tailing, and this driver you happened to get is, if anything worse. If you insist on tailing Joe, okay, we'll put him in the cab and let them go ahead, and you ride with me and I'll show you how it's done."

"Yeah?" the menace croaked. "Show her how what's done?"

"See that," I told her. "See the kind of mind he's got."

All her muscles were now under control. "You're smart as they come, aren't you?"

"That," I said, "you will learn more about as time goes on. I'm at least smarter than you are if you let that meter continue to tick. Pay him and come on."

She moved, so I stood aside and held the door while she got out. On the sidewalk she faced me and said, "You seem to be in charge of everything, so you pay him."

It was an unpleasant surprise, but I didn't hesitate, first, because I liked the way she was handling herself, and second, because all expenses would come out of the five grand anyway. So I parted with two bucks, took her elbow and steered her to the sedan, opened the front door and told Joe Groll, "Move over a little. There's room for three."

It was his turn to let his jaw hang. Apparently it was going to be prolonged, and he didn't budge, so I took her elbow again and escorted her around to the other side and told her, "Slide in under the wheel. I'd rather have you next to me anyhow."

She did so, and I got in and slammed the door. By the time I had got the engine started and rolled to the corner and turned downtown, neither of them had said a word.

"If I were you folks," I told them, "I would incorporate and call it the Greater New York Mutual Tailing League. I don't see how you keep track of who is following whom on any given day. Of course if one of you gets convicted of murder that will put a stop to it. You have now, however, the one good reason that I know of for getting married, the fact that a wife can't testify against a husband or vice versa." I swerved around a pushcart. "One thing you want to watch. Now that

157

Poor is dead, Helen will try to sell you the idea, Joe, that she was meeting him on the sly merely to keep him informed of anything Blaney seemed to be up to, and Joe will try to sell you the idea, Helen, that he was seeing Martha merely for that too. Now, of course, he can't marry her, at least not for a long time, because it would look suspicious, and he may want you for a stopgap. You should both be realistic—"

"Can it," Joe croaked. "We're not going there, where I said. Stop and let me out."

"Oh, yes we are." I stepped on it. "Stopgap or not, you are enjoying feeling her sit next to you as much as I am, and I could keep right on going to the foot of the rainbow. If you really wanted out, what was wrong with any of the stops for traffic lights? She can help us, and it won't hurt to have a witness. The idea is, Helen, we are bound for the Blaney and Poor office to go through the abditories. We think we hid something in them."

"What?" she demanded.

"We don't know. Maybe a detailed estimate in triplicate of what it would cost to kill Poor. Maybe a blueprint of the cigar. Even a rough sketch would help."

"That's ridiculous. You sound to me like a clown."

"Good. It is a well-known fact that clowns have the biggest and warmest hearts on record except mothers and three characters in books by Dickens. So if and when you get tired of being a stopgap, just give me a ring and—here we are."

I pulled over to the curb in front of Blaney and Poor's on Varick Street.

VII

That office was no place for a stranger to poke around in. It was on the first floor of a dingy old building in the middle of the block, with part of the factory, so Joe said, in the rear, and the rest on the second floor. As soon as we were inside and had the lights turned on, Helen sat in a chair at a desk and looked disdainful, but as the search went on I noticed she kept her eyes open. Joe tossed his hat and coat on a chair, got a screwdriver from a drawer, went to the typewriter on the desk Helen was sitting at, used the screwdriver, lifted out the typewriter roller, unscrewed an end of it and turned it vertical, and about four dozen dice rolled out. He held the open end of the roller so the light would hit it right, peered in, put the dice back in and screwed the end on, and put the roller back on the machine. His fingers were as swift and accurate as any I had ever seen. Even if I had known about it, I would have needed at least ten minutes for the operation; he took about three.

"Trick dice?" I asked him.

"They're just a stock item," he said, and went over to a door in the rear wall, opened it, took it off its hinges, leaned it against a desk, knelt on the floor, removed a strip from the bottom edge of the door—and out came about ten dozen lead pencils.

"Trick pencils?"

"When you press, perfume comes out," he said, and stretched out flat to look into the abditory.

I thought I might as well help with the doors and ambled over to open one in another wall that would probably be to a closet. I grabbed the knob and turned, and something darted out and banged me on the shin so that almost anyone but me would have screamed in pain. I uttered a word or two. The piece of wood that had hit me had gone back into place and was part of the door again.

"That shouldn't have been left connected," Helen said, trying not to look as if she wanted to giggle.

I saw no reason to reply. My shin feeling as it did, I thought it wouldn't hurt to see if the skin was broken and started to lift my foot to a chair, but the light was dim because the ones in that part of the room hadn't been turned on, so I stepped to the wall and flipped a switch. A stream of water, a thin stream but with plenty of pressure, came out of the wall and hit me just below the right eye. I leaped to one side and used more and better words.

"That's interesting," Helen said. "Some customers say that the person won't be standing in the right place, but you were, exactly. A person not as tall as you would get it right in the eye."

"You are," I told her grimly.

"I am what?"

"Not as tall as me."

"Oh, I have better sense."

Only a female idiot would have put it on a basis of sense. Joe, who had put the door back up and was lying on the floor again with his head stuck under a desk, called to me, "Maybe you hadn't better touch things."

"Thanks for the suggestion." I went to a chair at the end of the desk he was under and asked, "What happens if I sit on this?"

"Nothing. That one's okay."

I sat and became strictly a spectator, after wiping my face and neck and inspecting my shin. Joe continued his tour of the abditories, which were practically everywhere, in desk lamps, chair legs, water cooler, ash trays, even one in the metal base of a desk calendar that was on a big desk in the corner. It was while he had that one open, jiggling things out of it, that I heard him mutter, "This is a new one on me." He walked over and put something on the desk in front of Helen and asked her, "What is that thing, do you know?"

She picked it up, inspected it, and shook her head. "Haven't the faintest idea."

"Let me see." I got up and went over, and Helen handed it to me. The second I saw it I stopped being casual inside, but I tried to keep the outside as before. It was a long thin metal capsule, about three-quarters of an inch long and not over an eighth of an inch in diameter, smooth all over, with no seam or opening, except at one end where a thread came through, a dark brown medium-sized thread as long as my index finger.

I grunted. "Where did you find it?"

"You saw me find it." Joe sounded either irritated or something else. "In that calendar on Blaney's desk."

"Oh, that's Blaney's desk. How many, just this one?"

"No, several." Joe went to Blaney's desk and then came back to us. "Three more. Four altogether."

I took them from him and compared. They were all the same. I regarded Helen's attractive face. She looked interested. I regarded Joe's handsome face if you didn't count the ears. He looked more interested.

"I think," I said, "that it was one of these things that was in the cigar that Poor never smoked. What do you think?"

Joe said, "I think we can damn soon find out. Give me one." He had a gleam in his eye.

I shook my head. "The idea doesn't appeal to me." I looked at my wrist. "Quarter to nine. Mr. Wolfe is in the middle of dinner. The proper thing is for you to take these objects to the police, but they're likely to feel hurt because you didn't tell them about the abditories when they were here. We can't interrupt Mr. Wolfe's dinner, even with a phone call, so I suggest that I buy you a meal somewhere, modest but nutritious, and then we all three go and deliver these gadgets, calendar included, to him. He may want to ask some questions."

"You take them to him," Joe said. "I think I'll go home."

"I think I'll go home too," Helen said.

"No. Nothing doing. You'll just follow each other and get all confused again. If I take these things to Wolfe without taking you he'll fly into a temper and phone the police to go get you. Not to flatter myself, wouldn't you prefer to come with me?"

Helen said in the nastiest possible tone, "I don't have to eat at the same table with him."

Joe said, trying to match her tone but failing because he wasn't a female, "If you did I wouldn't eat."

Which was a lot of organic fertilizer. I took them to Gallagher's, where they not only ate at the same table but devoured hunks of steak served from the same platter. It was a little after ten when we got to Nero Wolfe's place on Thirty-fifth Street.

VIII

Wolfe was seated behind his desk, with the evening beer—one empty bottle and two full ones—on a tray in front of him. Joe Groll, in the red leather chair, also had a bottle and glass on the check-writing table beside him. Helen Vardis would have made a good cheesecake shot over by the big globe in an upholstered number that Wolfe himself sometimes used. I was at my own

161

desk, as usual, with my oral report all finished, watching Wolfe inspect the workmanship of the removable bottom of the desk calendar.

He put it down, picked up one of the metal capsules with its dangling thread and gave it another look, put that down too, and turned his half-closed eyes on Joe.

"Mr. Groll."

"Yes, sir."

"I don't know how much sense you have. If you have slightly more than your share, you must realize that if I hand these things to the police with Mr. Goodwin's story, they will conclude that you are a liar. They will ask, why did you wait until witnesses were present to explore those hiding places? Why did you think they were worth exploring at all? Is it even remotely credible that Mr. Blaney, after preparing that murderous box of cigars, would leave these things there on his desk in a hiding place that a dozen people knew about? They will have other questions, but that's enough to show that they will end by concluding that you put the capsules in the calendar yourself. Where did you get them?"

"But listen," Helen Vardis spoke up, "those abditor—"

"Miss Vardis! Please. I don't want to hear that word again! Mr. Goodwin used it repeatedly because he knew it would annoy me, but I don't have to stand it from strangers and I won't. I'm speaking to Mr. Groll. Well, sir?"

Joe said firmly, "I wouldn't know about how much sense I've got, but it happened exactly the way you've heard it. As for my waiting for witnesses, I didn't. I only waited until I was sure Blaney was out of range, up at his Westchester place, and then Goodwin was there and I asked him to come along on the spur of the moment. As for its being remotely credible what you said, there's nothing Blaney wouldn't do because he's crazy. He's a maniac. You don't know him, so you don't know that."

Wolfe grunted. "The devil I don't. I do know that. How long have those hiding places been in existence?"

"Some of them for years. Some are more recent."

Wolfe tapped the desk calendar with a finger. "How long has this been there?"

"Oh—" Joe considered. "Four or five years. It was there before I got in the Army. Look here, Mr. Wolfe, you seem to forget that when I saw those things tonight I had no idea what they were and I still haven't. You seem to know they're the same as the loads in those cigars, and if you do okay, but I don't."

"Neither do I."

"Then what the hell? Maybe they're full of Chanel Number Five or just fresh air."

Wolfe nodded. "I was coming to that. If I show them to Mr. Cramer he'll take them away from me, and also he'll arrest you as a material witness, and I may possibly need you. We'll have to find out for ourselves."

He pushed a button, and in a moment Fritz entered. Wolfe asked him, "Do you remember that metal percolator that someone sent us and we were fools enough to try?"

"Yes, sir."

"Did you throw it out?"

"No, sir, it's in the basement."

"Bring it here, please."

Fritz went. Wolfe picked up a capsule and frowned at it and then turned to me. "Archie. Get me a piece of newspaper, the can of household oil, and a piece of string."

Under the circumstances I would have preferred to go out for a walk, but there was a lady present who might need protection, so I did as I was told. When I got back Fritz was there with the percolator, which was two-quart size, made of thick metal. We three men collected at Wolfe's desk to watch the preparations, but Helen stayed in her chair. With my scissors Wolfe cut a strip of newspaper about two by eight inches, dropped oil on it and rubbed it in with his finger, and rolled it tight into a long, thin, oiled wick. Then he held one end of it against the end of the capsule thread, overlapping a little, and Joe Groll, ready with the piece of string, tied them together. Wolfe opened the lid of the percolator.

"No," Joe objected. "That might stop it. Anyhow, we don't want this glass here."

He finished the job with his swift sure fingers, while Wolfe and Fritz and I watched. Removing the glass cap and the inside contraption from the percolator, he lowered the capsule through the hole, hanging on to the free end of the oiled wick with one hand while with the other he stuffed a scrap of newspaper in the hole just tight enough to keep the wick from slipping on through. Wolfe nodded approvingly and leaned back in his chair. About two inches of the wick was protruding.

"Put it on the floor." Wolfe pointed. "Over there."

Joe moved, taking a folder of matches from his pocket, but I intercepted him. "Wait a minute. Gimme." I took the percolator. "The rest of you go in the hall. I'll light it."

Fritz went, and so did Helen, but Joe merely backed to a corner and Wolfe didn't move from his chair.

I told Wolfe, "I saw Poor's face and you didn't. Go in the hall."

"Nonsense. That little thing?"

"Then I'll put a blanket over it."

"No. I want to see it."

"So do I," Joe said. "What the hell. I'll bet it's a dud."

I shrugged. "I hope Helen has had a course in first aid." I put the percolator on the floor over by the couch, about five paces from Wolfe's desk, lit a match and applied it to the end of the wick, and stood back and watched. An inch of the wick burned in three seconds. "See you at the hospital," I said cheerily, and beat it to the hall, leaving the door open a crack to see through.

It may have been ten seconds, but it seemed like three times that, before the bang came, and it was a man-size bang, followed immediately by another but different kind of bang. Helen grabbed my arm, but not waiting to enjoy that I swung the door open and stepped through. Joe was still in the corner, looking surprised. Wolfe had twisted around in his chair to gaze at a bruise in the plaster of the wall behind him.

"The percolator lid," he muttered. "It missed me."

"Yeah." I moved across to observe angles and directions. "By about an inch." I stopped to pick up the percolator lid, bent out of shape. "This would have felt good on your skull."

Fritz and Helen were back in, and Joe came over with the percolator in his hand. "Feel it," he said. "Hot. Look how it's twisted. Some pill, that is. Dynamite or TNT would never do that, not that amount. I wonder what's in it?" He sighed. "Do you smell anything? I don't."

"It's outrageous," Wolfe declared. I looked at him in surprise. Instead of being relaxed and thankful for his escape, he was sitting straight in his chair, which meant he was ready to pop with fury. "That thing nearly hit me in the head. This settles it. Against Mr. Poor there may have been a valid grievance. Against me, none."

"Well, for God's sake." I regarded him without approval. "That's illogical. Nobody aimed it at you. Didn't I tell you to go in the hall? However, if it made you mad enough to do a little work, fine, here's Joe and Helen, you can start on them."

"No." He got to his feet. "I'm going to bed." He bowed to Helen. "Good night, Miss Vardis." He tilted his head a hundredth of an inch at Joe. "Good night, sir. Archie, put these remaining capsules in the safe." He marched to the door and was gone.

"Quite a guy," Joe remarked. "He didn't bat an eye when that thing went off and the lid flew past his ear."

"Yeah," I growled. "He has fits. He's having one now. Instead of taking you two apart and turning you inside out, which is what he should have done, he didn't even tell you where to head in. Do you tell the police about tonight or not? I would say, for the present, not. Come on. Taxis are hard to find around here, and I've got to put the car away anyhow. I'll drop you somewhere."

We went. When I got back, some time later, I made a little discovery. Opening the safe to follow my custom of checking the cash last thing at night, I found two hundred bucks gone and an entry in the book for that amount in Wolfe's handwriting which said, "Saul Panzer, advance on expenses."

So anyhow Saul was working.

IX

Friday morning, having nothing else to do, I solved the case. I did it with cold logic. Everything fitted perfectly, and all I needed was enough evidence for a jury. Presumably that was what Saul Panzer was getting. I do not intend to put it all down here, the way I worked it out, because first it would take three full pages, and second I was wrong. Anyway I had it solved when, a little before nine o'clock, I was summoned to Wolfe's room and given an errand to perform with detailed instructions. It sent me to Twentieth Street, so I went to the garage for the car and headed south.

I would just as soon have dealt with one of the underlings, but Cramer himself was in his office and said to bring me in. As I sat down he whirled his chair a quarter turn, folded his arms, and asked conversationally; "What have you two liars got cooked up now?"

I grinned at him. "Why don't you call Wolfe a liar to his face someday? Do it while I'm there." I took two of the capsules, with threads attached, from my vest pocket, put them on his desk, and inquired, "Do you need any more of these?"

He picked one of them up and gave it a good look, then the other one, put them in a drawer of his desk, folded his arms again, and looked me in the eye to shrivel me.

"All right," he said quietly. "Go on. They came in the mail, in a package addressed to Wolfe with letters cut out of a magazine."

"No, sir, not at all. Where I spent the night last night I was idly running my fingers through her lovely hair and felt something, and there they were." Cramer was strictly a family man and had stern ideas. Seeing I had him blushing, I went on, "Actually it was like this."

I told him the whole story, straight and complete.

He had questions, both during the recital and at the end, and I answered what I could. The one I had expected him to put first, he saved till the last.

"Well," he said, "for the present we'll assume that I believe you. You know what that amounts to, but we'll assume it. Even so, how are you on figures? How much are two and one?"

"I'm pretty good. Two plus one plus one equals four."

"Yes? Where do you get that second plus one?"

"So you can add," I conceded. "Mr. Wolfe thought maybe you couldn't. However, so can we. Four capsules were found. Two are there in your drawer. One, as I told you, was used in a scientific experiment in Wolfe's office and damn near killed him. He's keeping the other one for the Fourth of July."

"Like hell he is. I want it."

"Try and get it." I stood up. "Search warrant, subpoena, replevin, riot squad, tear gas, shoot the works. Standing in with G-2 as he does, he could get a carload of those things if he wanted them, but apparently he has taken a liking to this one nice bright little capsule. My God, you're hard to please. Your men search Blaney and Poor's without finding a single abditory, and I had to go and do it for you, and we're splitting fifty-fifty on the capsules. And you beef. May I go now?"

"Beat it. I'll get it."

I turned with dignity and went.

When I got back to Wolfe's Fritz met me in the hall to tell me there was a woman in the office, and when I entered I found it was Martha Poor.

I sat down at my desk and told her, "Mr. Wolfe will be engaged until eleven o'clock." I glanced at my wrist. "He'll be down in forty minutes."

She nodded. "I know. I'll wait."

She didn't look exactly bedraggled, nor would I say pathetic, but there was certainly nothing of the man-eater about her. She seemed older than she had on Tuesday. Anyone could have told at a glance that she was having trouble, but whether it was bereavement or bankruptcy was indicated neither by her clothes nor her expression. She merely made you feel like going up to her, maybe putting your hand on her shoulder or patting her on the arm, and asking, "Anything I can do?" It occurred to me that if she had been old enough to be my mother there would have been no question about how I felt, but she positively was not. If I had

167

wanted to pass the time by deciding what I might want her for when she stopped being in trouble, it would not have been for a mother.

Of course, since at that time I still had the case solved, and all I needed was evidence, there were about a dozen things I would have liked to ask her, but it seemed advisable to wait and let Wolfe do it. I reached that conclusion while I was sitting with my back to her, entering plant germination records, and that reminded me of a minor point I hadn't covered. I went to the kitchen and asked Fritz if he had told Wolfe who had come to see him, and Fritz said he hadn't, he had left that to me. So I returned to the office, buzzed the plant rooms, got Wolfe, and told him, "Returned from mission. I gave them to Cramer himself, and he says he'll get the other one. Mrs. Poor is down here waiting to see you."

"Confound that woman. Send her away."

"But she—"

"No. I know what she wants. I studied her. She wants to know what I'm doing to earn that money. Tell her to go home and read that receipt."

The line died. I swung my chair around and told Martha, "Mr. Wolfe says for you to go home and read the receipt."

She stared. "What?"

"He thinks you came to complain because he isn't earning the money your husband paid him, and the idea of having to earn money offends him. It always has."

"But—that's ridiculous. Isn't it?"

"Certainly it is." I fought back the impulse to step over and pat her on the shoulder. "But my advice is to humor him, much as I enjoy having you here. Nobody alive can handle him but me. If he came down and found you here he would turn around and walk out. If you have anything special to say, tell me and I'll tell him. He'll listen to me because he has to, or fire me, and he can't fire me because then he would never do any work at all and would eventually starve to death."

"I shouldn't think—" She stopped and stood up. She took a step toward the door, then turned and said, "I
168

shouldn't think a cold-blooded murder is something to joke about."

I had to fight back the impulse again. "I'm not joking," I declared. "Plain facts. What did you want to say to him?"

"I just wanted a talk with him. He hasn't come to see me. Neither have you." She tried to smile, but all she accomplished was to start her lip quivering. She stopped it. "You haven't even phoned me. I don't know what's happening. The police asked me about two of my hairs being in that box of cigars, and I suppose they have told Mr. Wolfe about it, and I don't even know what he thinks or what he told the police . . ."

I grinned at her. "That's easy. He made a speech to the jury, demonstrating that those hairs in the box were evidence that you did not kill your husband." I went to her and put a hand on her arm, like a brother. "Listen, lady. Isn't the funeral this afternoon?"

"Yes."

"Okay, go and have the funeral, that's enough for you for one day. Leave the rest to me. I mean, if anything occurs that it would help you to know about, I'll see that you know. Right?" She didn't pull anything corny like grasping my hand with hers firm and warm or gazing at me with moist eyes filled with trust. She did meet my eyes, but only long enough to say "Thank you, Mr. Goodwin," and turned to go. I went to the front door and let her out.

After Wolfe came down the relations between us were nothing to brag about. Apparently he had nothing to offer, and I was too sore to start in on him. I had brought him Helen and Joe, and except for having fun with that capsule like a kid with a firecracker, he hadn't bothered to disturb one cell of his celebrated brain. Martha had come on her own, and he wouldn't even see her. As for Blaney, I had to admit I couldn't blame him much on that, but the fact remained that he had walked out without doing a lick of work.

He passed the time until lunch going through catalogues, and at two-thirty P.M., with a veal cutlet and half a bushel of Fritz's best mixed salad stowed in the hold, he returned to the office and resumed with catalogues. That got interrupted before long, but not by me. The bell rang, and I went to the front and it was Saul Panzer. I took him to the office.

Wolfe greeted him and then told me, "Archie. Go up and help Theodore with the pollen lists."

There was nothing new about it, but that didn't make me like it any better. When the day finally comes that I tie Wolfe to a stake and shoot him, one of the fundamental reasons will be his theory that the less I know the more I can help, or to put it another way, that everything inside my head shows on my face. It only makes it worse that he doesn't really believe it. He merely can't stand it to have anybody keep up with him at any time on any track. I am being fair about it. I admit that even under ideal circumstances it wouldn't happen very often, but it would ruin a good meal for him if it ever happened at all.

I did my best with Theodore and the pollen lists, not wanting to take it out on them. The conference with Saul seemed to be comprehensive, since a full hour passed before the house phone in the potting room buzzed. Theodore answered it, and told me that I was wanted downstairs.

When I got there Saul was gone. I had a withering remark prepared, thinking to open up with it, but had to save it for some other time. Wolfe was seated behind his desk, leaning back with his eyes closed, and his lips were moving, pushing out and then in again, out and in. . . .

So I sat down and kept my mouth shut. The brain had actually got on the job, and I knew better than to make remarks, withering or not, during the performance of miracles. The first result, which came in ten or twelve minutes after I entered, did not however seem to be very miraculous. He opened his eyes halfway, grunted, and muttered, "Archie. Yesterday you showed me an article in a paper about a man's body found in an orchard near White Plains, but I didn't look at it. Now I want it."

"Yes, sir. There was more this morning—"

"Have they identified the body?"

"No, sir. The head was smashed—"

"Get it."

I obeyed. Newspapers were kept in the office for three days. I opened it to the page and handed it to him. He would read a newspaper only one way, holding it out wide open, no folding, with his arms stretched. I had never tried to get him to do it more intelligently because it was the only strenuous exercise he ever got and was therefore good for him. He finished the Thursday piece and asked for Friday's, and finished that.

Then he told me, "Get the district attorney of Westchester County. What's his name? Fraser?"

"Right." I got busy with the phone. I had no trouble getting the office, but then they gave me the usual line about Mr. Fraser being in conference and I had to put on pressure. Finally the elected person said hello.

Wolfe took it. "How do you do, Mr. Fraser. Nero Wolfe. I have something to give you. That body found in an orchard Wednesday evening with the head crushed—has it been identified?"

Fraser was brusque. "No. What—"

"Please. I'm giving you something. Put this down. Arthur Howell, nine one four West Seventy-eighth Street, New York. He worked for the Beck Products Corporation of Basston, New Jersey. They have an office at six two East Forty-second Street, New York. His dentist was Lewis Marley, six nine nine Park Avenue, New York. That should help. Try that. In return for this, I would appreciate it very much if you will have me notified the moment the identification is made. Did you get it all down?"

"Yes. But what—"

"No, sir. That's all. That's all you'll get from me until I get word of the identification."

There was some sputtering protest from the White Plains end, but it accomplished nothing. Wolfe hung up with a self-satisfied smirk on his big face, cleared his throat importantly, and picked up a catalogue.

I growled at him, "So it's in the bag. A complete stranger named Arthur Howell. After snitching the capsules from Beck Products and making the cigars and getting them into Poor's home God knows how, he was overcome by remorse and went to an orchard and took

171

his clothes off and lay down and ran a car over himself with radio control—"

"Archie. Shut up. We are ready to act in any case, but it will make things a little simpler if that corpse proves to be Mr. Howell, so it is worth waiting for a report on it." He glanced at the clock, which said seven minutes to four, and put the catalogue down. "We might as well prepare it now. Get that capsule from the safe."

I thought to myself, this time it may not miss him, but as for me, I'm going outdoors. However, it appeared that he was going to try some new gag instead of repeating with the percolator. By the time I got the capsule from the safe and convoyed it to him, he had taken two articles from a drawer and put them on his desk. One was a roll of Scotch tape. The other was a medium-sized photograph of a man, mounted on gray cardboard. I gave it a glance, then picked it up and did a thorough job of looking. It was unquestionably Eugene R. Poor.

"Goody," I said enthusiastically. "No wonder you're pleased. Even if Saul had to pay two hundred bucks for it—"

"Archie. Let me have that. Here, hold this thing."

I helped. What I was to hold was the capsule, flat on the cardboard near a corner, while he tore off a piece of tape and fastened it there. When he lifted the photo and jiggled it to see if the fastening was firm, the thread dangled over Poor's right eye.

"Put it in an envelope and in the safe," he said, glanced at the clock, and made for the hall and the elevator.

That was all for the present. I sat at my desk and went over the case again, testing my logic point by point. The conclusion I reached an hour later was that there were two distinct kinds of logic, Wolfe's and mine, and that they were destined to clash. I wasn't dumb enough not to have a general idea of where his was headed for, but where he got the notion that we were ready to act was way beyond me. It looked to me as if we were barely ready to start wondering what to do.

At six o'clock he returned to the office, rang for Fritz

to bring beer, and took up where he had left off with the catalogues. At eight o'clock Fritz summoned us to dinner. At nine-thirty we returned to the office. At a quarter to ten a phone call came from District Attorney Fraser. The body had been identified. It was Arthur Howell. An assistant district attorney and a pair of detectives were on their way to Thirty-fifth Street to ask Wolfe, how come and would he please supply all necessary details, including the present address of the murderer.

Wolfe hung up, leaned back and sighed, and muttered at me, "Archie. You'll have to pay a call on Mrs. Poor."

I objected, "She's probably in bed, tired out. The funeral was today."

"It can't be helped. Saul will go with you."

I stared. "Saul?"

"Yes. He's up in my room asleep. He didn't get to bed last night. You will take her that photograph of her husband. You should leave as soon as possible, before that confounded Westchester lawyer gets here. I don't want to see him. Tell Fritz to bolt the door after you go. Ring my room and tell Saul to come down at once. Then I'll give you your instructions."

X

The appearance of the living room in the Poor apartment on Eighty-fourth Street was not the same as it had been when I had arrived there three evenings before. Not only was there no army of city employees present and no man of the house with his face gone huddled on the floor, but the furniture had been moved around. The chair Poor had sat in when he lit his last cigar was gone, probably to the cleaners on account of spots, the table Cramer had used for headquarters had been shifted to the other side of the room, and the radio had been moved to the other end of the couch.

Martha Poor was sitting on the couch, and I was on a chair I had pulled around to face her. She was wearing something that wasn't a bathrobe and wasn't ex-

173

actly a dress, modest, with sleeves and only a proper amount of throat showing.

"I'm here under orders," I told her. "I said this morning that if anything happened that it would help you to know about I'd see that you knew, but this isn't it. This is different. Nero Wolfe sent me with orders. I just want to make that clear. Item number one is to hand you this envelope and invite you to look at the contents."

She took it from me. With steady fingers, slow-moving rather than hurried, she opened the flap and pulled out the photograph.

I informed her, "That decoration may look like something by Dali, but it was Nero Wolfe's idea. I am not authorized to discuss it or the picture from any angle, just there it is, except to remark that it is a very good likeness of your husband. I only saw him that one time, the other afternoon at the office, but of course I had a long and thorough look at him. Wednesday we could have sold that photo to a newspaper for a nice amount, but of course we didn't have it Wednesday."

She had put the photo beside her on the couch and was pinching an edge of the cardboard between her index finger and thumbnail, with the nail sinking in. She was looking straight at me. The muscles of her throat had tightened, which no doubt accounted for the change in her voice when she spoke.

"Where did you get it?"

I shook my head. "Out of bounds. As I said, I'm under orders. Item number two is just a piece of information to the effect that a man named Saul Panzer is out in the back hall on this floor, standing by the door of the service elevator. Saul is not big but he just had a nap and is alert. Number three: that naked body found up in Westchester with the head smashed by running a car over it, in an orchard not more than ten minutes' drive from either Monty's Tavern or Blaney's place, has been identified as formerly belonging to a man named Arthur Howell, an employee of the Beck Products Corporation."

Her eyes hadn't moved. I hadn't even seen the lashes blink. She said in a faraway voice, "I don't know

174

why you tell me about that. Arthur Howell? Did you say Arthur Howell?"

"Yep, that's right. Howell, Arthur. Head flattened to a pancake, but enough left for the dentist. As for telling you about it, I'm only obeying orders." I glanced at my wrist. "Number four: it is now twenty past ten. At a quarter to eleven I am supposed either to arrive back at the office or phone. If I do neither, Nero Wolfe will phone Inspector Cramer and then here they'll come. Not as many as Tuesday evening I suppose, because they won't need all the scientists, but plenty."

I stopped, still meeting her eye, and then went on, "Let's see. Photo and capsule, Saul out back, Howell, cops at quarter to eleven . . . that's all."

She got up, with the photo in her hand, and started for a door to the right, the one she had retreated through Tuesday when Blaney had arrived on the scene.

It was up to me to decide. If she wanted to be alone to get her mind arranged, or anything else arranged, that was all right with me, but the one detail which I thought had not been sufficiently considered was fire escapes. So although I would have much preferred to stay where I was, I went along.

That game of follow the leader was one of my experiences that can stay unique and suit me fine. She might have been a deaf-and-dumb renting agent showing me the apartment, and me a deaf-and-dumb renting prospective tenant. First we did the master bedroom, her in front and me right behind. She went and opened a closet door, looked in a moment, and shut it again. Then she crossed to another door that was standing open. I had never seen a fire escape with an entrance through a bathroom window, but I thought it wouldn't hurt to look so I did. Seeing it was okay, I backed out and she shut the door, staying inside. I went to a window and frowned out at the dark for maybe three minutes, and apparently I forgot to breathe, for when the door opened and she came out I pulled in enough oxygen to fill a barrel. Observing that she no longer was carrying the photograph, I let her go on being it. Her next destination was the back door, leading from the kitchen to the service hall. With me at her elbow, she pulled the door wide open, and we were both looking at Saul, standing there reading a newspaper.

He turned his head our way, and I said, "Hello, Saul."

He said, "Hello, Archie."

She closed the door, not letting it bang, and went by way of the dining room back to the living room and on to the front foyer. If this seems crazy to you reading about it, that's nothing to what it seemed to me helping do it. Not wanting any scene in the public hall, I slipped ahead of her in the foyer and stood with my back against the entrance door, and she simply turned around and re-entered the living room. I hadn't the dimmest idea then whether she was merely a rat in a cage and acting like one, or what, and I haven't now. But I wasn't going to have to phone Nero Wolfe that she had climbed down a fire escape and would he please tell the police to start looking, so when she kept going until she was in the master bedroom again I was right there.

She hadn't uttered one word since she had asked me if I had said Arthur Howell, but now she did. When she turned, in the middle of the room, near the foot of the big double bed where she had presumably slept with her husband, I thought she was going to take hold of me, but all she did was stand in front of me, about eight inches away, looking up at me. She came about up to my chin, that was all. She wasn't tall.

"Archie Goodwin," she said. "You think I'm terrible, don't you? You think I'm an awful woman, bad clear through. Don't you?"

"I'm not thinking, lady. I'm just an errand boy." The funny thing was that if at any moment up to then I had made a list of the ten most beautiful women she would not have been on.

"You've had lots of experience," she said, her head back to look up at me. "You know what women are like. I knew you did when you put your hand on my arm yesterday. You know I'm a man's woman, but it has to be the right man. Just one man's, forever." She started to smile, and her lip began to quiver, and she stopped it. "But I didn't find the man until it was too

176

late. I didn't find him until you put your hand on my arm yesterday. You could have had me then, forever yours, you could have me now if anything like that was possible. I mean—we could go away together—now you wouldn't have to promise anything—only you could find out if you want me forever too—the way I want you—"

She lifted her hand and touched me, just a touch, the tips of her fingers barely brushing my sleeve.

I jerked back.

"Listen," I said, with my voice sounding peculiar, so I tried to correct it. "You are extremely good, no question about it, but as you say, it's too late. You are trying to go to bat when your side already has three out in the ninth, and that's against the rules. I'll hand it to you that you are extremely good. When you turn it on it flows. But in seven minutes now Nero Wolfe will be phoning the police, so you'd better fix your hair. You'll be having your picture taken."

She hauled off and smacked me in the face. I barely felt it and didn't even move my hands.

"I hate men," she said through her teeth. "God, how I hate men!"

She turned and walked to the bathroom, and entered and closed the door.

I didn't know whether she had gone to fix her hair or what, and I didn't care. Instead of crossing to the window and standing there without breathing, as I had done before, I sat down on the edge of the bed and did nothing but breathe. I suppose I did actually know what was going to happen. Anyhow, when it happened, when the noise came, not nearly as loud as it had been in Wolfe's office because then the capsule had been inside a metal percolator, I don't think I jumped or even jerked. I did not run, but walked, to the bathroom door, opened it and entered.

Less than a minute later I went to the back door in the kitchen and opened that and told Saul Panzer, "All over. She stuck it in her mouth and lit the fuse. You get out. Go and report to Wolfe. I'll phone the cops."

"But you must be—I'll stay—"

"No, go on. Step on it. I feel fine."

At noon the next day, Saturday, I was getting fed up with all the jabber because I had a question or two I wanted to ask myself. Cramer had come to Nero Wolfe's office prepared to attack from all sides at once, bringing not only Sergeant Purley Stebbins but also a gang of civilians consisting of Helen Vardis, Joe Groll, and Conroy Blaney. Blaney had not been let in. On that Wolfe would not budge. Blaney was not to enter his house. The others had all been admitted and were now distributed around the office, with Cramer, of course, in the red leather chair. For over half an hour he and Wolfe had been closer to getting locked in a death grip than I had ever seen them before.

Wolfe was speaking. "Then arrest me," he said. "Shut up, get a warrant, and arrest me."

Cramer, having said about all an inspector could say, merely glared.

"Wording the charge would be difficult," Wolfe murmured. When he was maddest he murmured. "I have not withheld evidence, or obstructed justice, or shielded the guilty. I thought it possible that Mrs. Poor, confronted suddenly with that evidence, would collapse and confess."

"Nuts," Cramer said wearily. "How about confronting me with the evidence? Instead of evidence, what you confront me with is another corpse. And I know"—he tapped the chair arm with a stiff finger—"exactly why. The only evidence you had that was worth a damn was that photograph of Arthur Howell. If you had turned it over to me—"

"Nonsense. You already had a photograph of Arthur Howell. Several of them. The Beck Products Corporation people gave them to you on Thursday. So they told Saul Panzer. What good would one more do you?"

"Okay." Cramer was in a losing fight and knew it. "But I didn't know that Howell had come to see you on Tuesday with Mrs. Poor, passing himself off as her husband. Dressed in the same kind of suit and shirt and tie that Poor was wearing that day. Only you and Goodwin knew that."

"I knew it. Mr. Goodwin didn't. He thought it was a photograph of Mr. Poor."

"Protecting the help, huh?" Cramer snorted incredulously. "Anyhow, you knew it, and you knew it sewed her up, and you knew if she was arrested and came to trial you would have to go to court and testify, and you don't like to leave home and you don't like what there is to sit on in a courtroom, so you arrange it otherwise, and I'll be damned if anyone has appointed you judge, jury, district attorney, and the police force all in one."

Wolfe's shoulders moved an eighth of an inch up and down. "As I said, get a warrant, but watch the wording."

Cramer glared. A noise like a giggle came from the direction of Helen Vardis, and Joe Groll, being perched on the arm of her chair and therefore close enough, put his hand over hers. Apparently the days when they had taken turns following each other were only a memory.

I put in an entry. "Excuse me, but when you gentlemen finish the shadow-boxing I would like to ask a question." I was looking at Wolfe. "You say you knew Poor wasn't Poor. When and how?"

Of course Wolfe faked. He sighed as if he were thinking now this is going to be an awful bore. Actually he was always tickled stiff to show how bright he was.

His eyes came to me. "Wednesday evening you told me that Mr. Poor smoked ten to fifteen cigars a day. Thursday Mr. Cramer said the same thing. But the man that came here Tuesday, calling himself Poor, didn't even know how to hold a cigar, let alone smoke one."

"He was nervous."

"If he was he didn't show it, except with the cigar. You saw him. It was a ludicrous performance and he should never have tried it. When I learned that Mr. Poor was a veteran cigar smoker, the only question was who had impersonated him in this office? And the complicity of Mrs. Poor was obvious, especially with the added information, also furnished by Mr. Cramer, that no photograph of Mr. Poor was available. There are photographs of everybody nowadays. Mrs. Poor was an ass. She was supremely an ass when she selected me to bamboozle. She wanted to establish the assumption that Mr. Blaney was going to kill Mr. Poor. That was intelligent. She did not want to take her counterfeit Mr. Poor to the police, for fear someone there might be acquainted with the real Mr. Poor. That was also intelligent. But it was idiotic to choose me as the victim."

"She hated men," I remarked.

Wolfe nodded. "She must have had a low opinion of men. In order to get what she wanted, which presumably was something like half a million dollars—counting her husband's fortune, the insurance money, and a half share in the business after Mr. Blaney had been executed for the murder of Mr. Poor—she was willing to kill three men, two by direct action and one indirectly. Incidentally, except for the colossal blunder of picking on me she was not a fool."

"The hell she wasn't," Cramer growled. "With all that trick set-up? She was absolutely batty."

"No, sir." Wolfe shook his head. "She was not. Go back over it. She didn't manufacture the trick set-up out of her head, she simply used what she had. On a certain day she found herself with these ingredients at hand. One, the hostility between the partners in the business, amply corroborated by such details as Mr. Poor having Miss Vardis spy on Mr. Blaney, and Mrs. Poor herself having Mr. Groll do the same. Two, her acquaintance with a man named Arthur Howell, who had access to a supply of explosive capsules capable of concealment in a cigar, and who also sufficiently resembled her husband in build and general appearance except for the face itself, and she intended to take care of the face. Ten of your men, Mr. Cramer, kept at it for a week or so, can probably trace her association with Mr. Howell. They're good at that. Unquestionably it was those qualifications of Mr. Howell that suggested the details of her plan. She did not of course inform him that she hated men. Quite the contrary. She persuaded him to help her kill her husband, offering, presumably, a strong incentive."

"She was good at offering incentives," I declared. "She was good period. The way she pretended here, Tuesday afternoon, that she wanted Poor to skip it and go live in the country and grow roses, with her to cook and darn socks."

Wolfe nodded. "I admit she was ingenious. By the way, Mr. Groll, did she have an opportunity to conceal those four capsules in that desk calendar?"

"Yes," Joe said. "Helen and I were discussing that. She came there Tuesday to go with Poor to the rodeo, and she could have done it then. Anyway, she had keys, she could have done it any time."

"That was well conceived," Wolfe said approvingly. "That and the hairs in the box of cigars. She was preparing for all contingencies. Neither of those touches was meant for you, Mr. Cramer, but for a jury in case it ever got to that. She had sense enough to know what a good lawyer could do with complications of that sort. Will you gentlemen have some beer?"

"No," Cramer said bluntly. "I'll have a question. Poor wasn't here Tuesday afternoon?"

"No, sir. Arthur Howell was."

"Then where was he?"

"At the rodeo." Wolfe pushed a button, two pushes for beer. "Again Mrs. Poor was ingenious. Look at her schedule for Tuesday. She went to the Blaney and Poor office—what time, Mr. Groll?"

Helen answered. "She came around noon. They went to lunch together and then were going to the rodeo."

"Thank you. So all she had to do was to make some excuse and see that he went to the rodeo alone. It was an ideal selection—Madison Square Garden, that enormous crowd. Then she met Arthur Howell somewhere near, having arranged for him to be dressed as her husband was dressed, and brought him here. She was driving her car—or her husband's car. They left here a little before five o'clock. Between here and Forty-second Street he got out and went to Grand Central to take a train to White Plains. A woman who could persuade a man to help her kill her husband could surely persuade him to take a train to White Plains."

Fritz brought beer, and Wolfe opened a bottle and poured.

"Then she continued to Fiftieth Street and met her husband as he left the rodeo, and they drove to Westchester, having an appointment to see Mr. Blaney

181

at his place there. She talked her husband out of that, left him at a place called Monty's Tavern, drove somewhere, probably the White Plains railroad station, met Arthur Howell there as arranged, drove to an isolated spot probably previously selected, turned off the road into an orchard, killed Mr. Howell or knocked him unconscious with whatever she used for that purpose, removed his clothing, and ran the car over him to obliterate his face."

A noise came from Helen Vardis. She had obliterated her own face by covering it with her hands. That gave Joe an excuse to touch her again, which he did.

"Granted her basic premise," Wolfe went on, "she couldn't very well have been expected to let Arthur Howell continue to live. She would never have had a carefree moment. What if Mr. Goodwin or I had met him on the street? That thought should have occurred to him, but apparently something about Mrs. Poor had made him quit thinking. There are precedents. Since she was good at detail, I presume she spread his coat over his head so as to leave no telltale matter on her tires. What she then did with the clothing is no longer of interest, at least not to me."

He drank beer. "She proceeded. First to Mr. Blaney's place to make sure, by looking through windows, that he was alone there, so that she could safely say that she had gone to see him and couldn't find him. Again she was providing for all contingencies. If Arthur Howell's body was after all identified, known as that of a man who was with the Beck Products Corporation and had access to those capsules, it would help to have it established that Mr. Blaney had not been at home during the time that Arthur Howell had been killed. It wouldn't surprise me if a good search around Mr. Blaney's place discovered Mr. Howell's clothes concealed—no, that wouldn't do, since they were the same as Mr. Poor's. She wouldn't make that kind of mistake."

He emptied the glass. "The rest is anticlimax, though of course for her it was the grand consummation. She returned to Monty's Tavern, told her husband Mr. Blaney had not been at home, dined with him, drove back to New York and went to their apartment, and got him a nice fresh cigar from a new box. Everything worked perfectly. It sounds more complicated than it really was. Such details as making sure that no photographs of her husband would be available for the newspapers had no doubt been already attended to."

"That receipt you signed," Cramer growled.

"What? Oh. That gave her no difficulty. Arthur Howell gave the receipt to her, naturally, and she put it in her husband's pocket. That was important. It was probably the first thing she did after the cigar exploded."

"Meanwhile you've got the five thousand dollars."

"Yes, sir. I have."

"But Poor didn't pay it to you. You never saw Poor. You weren't hired by him. If you want to say Mrs. Poor paid it, do you take money from murderers?"

It was one of Cramer's feeblest attempts to be nasty, certainly not up to his standard.

Wolfe merely poured beer and said, "Pfui. Whether Mr. Poor paid me or not, he got his money's worth."

Try analyzing the logic of that. I can't.

ABOUT THE AUTHOR

REX STOUT, born in Kansas in 1886, has had an extremely varied career. After leaving the Navy in 1908, he became an itinerant bookkeeper and then worked as a sight-seeing guide, bookstore salesman, stablehand, and hotel manager. Later he devised and implemented a school banking system which was installed in four hundred cities and towns throughout the country. In 1927 he retired from the world of finance and began writing. His first Nero Wolfe novel, FER-DE-LANCE, appeared in 1934.

In 1941 Mr. Stout became chairman of the Writer's War Board, and in 1943 he was elected president of the Authors Guild. Since 1946 he has written more than twenty-eight Nero Wolfe books. Mr. Stout's titles include: BEFORE MIDNIGHT, THE FATHER HUNT, GAMBIT, MIGHT AS WELL BE DEAD, THREE WITNESSES, TROUBLE IN TRIPLICATE and PLEASE PASS THE GUILT. Mr. Stout and his wife, Pola, presently live in a house that straddles the New York-Connecticut line and contains three hundred plants.

NERO WOLFE

He's not much to look at and he'll never win the hundred yard dash, but for sheer genius at unraveling the tangled skeins of crime, he has no peer. His outlandish adventures make for some of the best mystery reading in paperback. He's the hero of these superb suspense stories.

BY REX STOUT

the grand master of detection

☐ TROUBLE IN TRIPLICATE	8456	(95¢)
☐ MIGHT AS WELL BE DEAD	8440	(95¢)
☐ GAMBIT	7697	(95¢)
☐ THREE WITNESSES	7149	(75¢)
☐ THE FATHER HUNT	6729	(75¢)

WHODUNIT?